Dedication

To Annette who was, and is, by my side at
all times; guiding me through the rough
patches, like she always has.

Twice Upon a Time

by
Andy Halpin

December 2013

Twice Upon A Time

2013

Published by Emu Ink Ltd
www.emuink.ie

Cover Art: Betty Mc Cormack
Design by Gwen Taylour

ISBN: 978-1-909684-34-8

Acknowledgements

To Betty McCormack, an artist from Bray who listened to my story and searched her archives. I owe a huge debt of gratitude to her for the wonderful cover, which features the old and long demolished Capitol Cinema, where Annette and I had our first date way back when.

To my family for their ongoing support in always being there for me, even when at times I may not have been there for them.

Finally to Emer Cleary at *Emu Ink* for all the help and support I received from her throughout the process. Also for her generosity of spirit in having the grace and courage to take the book on and make it what it is today.

Introduction

Twice Upon A Time is my fictitious attempt to hold onto something precious I lost, and should not be confused with reality. When Annette passed out of my life in April 2009 I was totally unprepared for the life I was then forced to lead. We had been together for almost forty four years and I depended (without fully realising how much) on Annette for almost everything in my life – companionship, friendly advice, guidance, a shoulder to cry on, encouragement, support for a renewal of confidence when I failed at something, and most of all, unconditional friendship, forgiveness and love.

With Annette's passing I was left without any of those things and I missed them so much.

When the enormity of the loss my family and I had suffered fully registered with me, and it did not do so for quite a while after her passing, I was shattered. I was confused and dazed by the unreality, as I saw it, of what had happened to us as a family and I was totally despondent at the way the life Annette and I had shared for so long had been suddenly obliterated and rendered almost as if it had never happened.

Forty four years of togetherness had been wiped out in a heartbeat and I was left with no one to turn to for an explanation. Annette had been the one I turned to for solace at times like this, but in my solitude I was bereft. I was rudderless and without any sense of direction as I faced into my old age alone.

We had been denied the opportunity of sailing gracefully (or disgracefully!) into the twilight of our years together, and I resented that, especially when I observed other couples of our vintage enjoying each other's companionship and thinking "that should be us." Although I still rejoiced for them in their happiness.

I tried so desperately, in every way I knew how, to bring Annette back into my life again so as to somehow be able to live out the remaining sunset years that had been denied to us.

One of the ways I tried to keep Annette alive was by writing about her. I started writing my recollections of our early years together, our meeting in Bray, our courtship and the process of falling in love, marrying and raising a family. It was never intended to be a book, it was, I believed, simply therapy – my way of keeping Annette with me in some shape or form in those lonely days after her passing. But as I wrote I found myself remembering things that were buried deep in my subconscious. People and places we had encountered on our journey through life were making themselves known to me once more in the writing, and I began to believe that Annette was helping me with these recollections, guiding me even, and a belief began to form in my mind that maybe, just maybe, I could write a book. The result of all that was *From Bray To Eternity*, a wholly factual memoir of the life we had shared since our first meeting in Bray in 1965. I published that book in 2012, in aid of the Bursary Fund for Young Musicians established in Annette's name, with the proceeds of a concert of her music, which was performed by her many friends in the Civic Theatre in Tallaght to mark the occasion of her first anniversary in 2010.

When "Bray" was finished I thought my time as an author was finished as well. I never intended writing another book, but I had experienced so much happiness, peace and comfort while writing, believing Annette was with me and helping me, that shortly after "Bray" was completed I began to miss the hours I had spent in the little back bedroom reprising our life on paper and I began to wonder if I could possibly do it all again, write another book with Annette as my ghost writer.

In the empty days after Annette passed out of my life I often wished and prayed, as I am sure many bereaved partners do, that we could do it all again, live our life all over again and undo the mistakes we made, avoid the hurts we caused each other from time to time, maybe even reach a time of no regrets.

There was a saying I had, which I often quoted to Annette when she questioned the practicality of something I wanted to try or do, "You can do anything in the movies," and I began to think a variation of that quote could be applied to a book, "You can write anything in a book."

Fortified by that thought that's exactly what I tried to do. Why could we not live our life all over again? Live it not in the reality of the here and now, but in fantasy on the pages of a book? And why not live it exactly the way we want it to be, with no complications and a happy ever after ending?

The book in your hand is a work of fiction, stimulated in part by events which occurred in my life and a desire, a compulsion even on my part, to keep that life, with Annette, going for as long as possible.

I believe it is true to say that most, if not all of us have, at some time or another wished to be given the chance to go back in time and undo or change something we regretted happening in this life; and in *Twice Upon A Time* I have given myself that chance. After all, you *can* write anything in a book.

Chapter one

I ONCE believed that when you lose someone you love, love like you never thought possible, your life changes so irreparably that any one single thing after that could never have a more profound effect – I was wrong.

I can still picture it. That sunny day in the Phoenix Park and me, a lonely old man, walking aimlessly through the crowds of dog walkers, picnickers and joggers; still stunned by the sudden onset of the illness that had taken my Annette away from me – despite it being a year previous. Thoughts of how helpless I had felt when it came to being there for her, comforting her and making her feel safe, raced through my mind, stabbing at my heart. The Cancer had really ambushed us and now I was condemned to live a new, lonely and incredibly empty life without her.

Every 'if only' came and passed through my mind, taunting me as they had done for twelve months. I still couldn't accept that I would never see her again and my pain was indescribable.

I had entered the Phoenix Park that day after getting off the Luas tram at Heuston Station and without ever planning or thinking it through I walked as far as the Hollow before turning back towards the People's Gardens at the North Circular Road entrance to the park.

I stood at the railings at the top of the hill, vacantly looking around the deserted park and I began to remember the times I was there when I was young, playing games with my brother, running up and down the steps and rolling down the hill. I stood looking down that very hill imagining the park filled with people, the ghosts of my childhood, and in my mind I was back there, a child again. I could see myself running and rolling and the visions and sounds of the present were replaced by visions and sounds of the past as my ghostly companions invited me to join them. I needed to. I needed an escape, anything to take my thoughts away from my pain. I wanted to live that life again, to be young again, and so, in a state of euphoria, I lay on the grass at the top of the hill, imagined myself with no worries or concerns and pushed myself forward and down.

I seemed to be spinning forever as alternately my eyes were filled with visions of the green grass and blue sky. Then, eventually, I stopped and lay motionless at the bottom of the hill with my eyes tightly shut and the sun, warm on my face.

Softly at first and then progressively louder I began to hear the sound of voices, children shouting and laughing as they played... and then that of footsteps.

I heard my name being called.

"Andrew, Andrew, come on we're going home now, your da will be in from work soon."

I sat up, opened my eyes and looked around the park, it was filled with people, real people, not those conjured up by the tormented mind that I had left at the top of the hill. As I struggled for breath I heard the voice call me again.

"Andrew, come on will you, we have to go home." I knew that voice, but no it couldn't be... I turned to see who was calling me and sure enough I saw her, my mother standing, holding my younger brother by the hand and looking down at me.

I then looked at myself, at my clothes, they were not the ones I had on me just a few moments ago. Then I noticed my hands, they were not the vein-ridden loose-skinned hands of an elderly man anymore, they were young and the skin was tight and clear. I stopped at my left hand – where was my wedding ring? I put my hands to my face and although I knew I had not shaved for a few days my face was soft and smooth to the touch, with not a trace of stubble.

I was a boy again.

Dressed in a pair of long brown corduroy trousers and a white open-necked shirt, with a pair of white, old-fashioned runners on my feet, I began to recognise the clothing of the young boy I used to be in the 60s. But I was baffled, what had happened to me? What had caused this change? Had I hit my head while spinning down the hill and was hallucinating? I sat where I was and tightly closed my eyes again expecting things to be back to normal when I opened them. Then I heard my mother's voice again, calling my name, and as I tried to raise myself from the ground I felt her tug on my shirt and I opened my eyes. I turned to face her – my long-dead mother, now a fifty-year-old woman once more and I was speechless.

"Did you not hear me calling you? It's late and we have to go, your da will be in from work," she said as she stood over me, still holding the sleeve of my shirt as my young brother stood beside her looking at me.

I was now confused and frightened by what was happening and I tried to pull away so she loosened her grip on my shirt. I stood looking at them, totally bewildered, my mother and my eleven-year-old brother who was a sixty-year-old man the last time I saw him. I was shocked and mystified by what was happening, and with what must have been a look of horror on my face I tried to run away, but my mother quickly gripped my shirt sleeve and held me close to her before saying; "Jesus, Mary and Joseph what's wrong with you Andrew?"

I could not speak. I froze as I stood looking at them and then at the people who had started to gather around us, attracted by my mother's reaction. They were all dressed in old-fashioned clothes, the women in flowery summer dresses with large white buttons down the front, and they all had old-fashioned hair styles, the men mostly in dark suits, white shirts and some with cloth caps while the young boys and girls were in short pants and shirts or light summer dresses.

"For God's sake Andrew what's wrong with you, did anyone do anything to you?" my mother asked as I stood in a state of utter confusion and terror.

"No," is all I could force out of my mouth, my voice sounded so strange!

"Then what's wrong with you?" she pleaded.

"I don't know."

All I knew was that a few moments before I was a sad, lonely sixty-five-year-old man, grieving the loss of his wife; and now it appeared I was a fifteen-year-old boy again.

When my mind began to comprehend what seemed the impossible had happened, that somehow I had been cast back in time, I composed myself and went with my mother and brother to the bus stop on Infirmary Road and got the old green double-decker C.I.E. bus to the corner of Berkley Road. What choice did I have? With the entrance at the back of the bus I watched in awe as the conductor stood, an air of importance about him, until it was time to get off.

We then walked the short distance to our tenement house, number fifty-five, Lower Wellington Street. It was fifty years since I had last seen or been in this house, indeed we would not be in it much longer; I remembered we moved out of it and into the new flats in Dominick Street in 1961 – so this had to be about 1960.

Chapter two

WHEN we climbed the six flights of stairs, to the rooms we occupied on the third floor, my father was already home from work. If I had the year correct he was then fifty three years of age and a kitchen porter in the Hibernian Hotel on Dawson Street, having previously worked in the Gresham Hotel on O'Connell Street. As he stood before me he seemed much smaller and thinner than I remembered. "Where were you?" he asked.

"We went to the park, Andrew didn't go into work today, he wasn't well this morning," my mother answered.

When I heard this I had to think for a moment, work? Where was I working? I still wasn't certain what year it was. There was an *Evening Herald* on the table so I quickly picked it up and looked at the date. It was Tuesday, September 13th, 1960, in which case I was working in *Burroughs & Watts*, Billiard Table makers on Mary Street.

"What was wrong with you?" My father was looking at me now.

With no idea what was wrong with me I looked at my mother.

"He was doing his gik all the time," my little brother laughed.

"That's all that rubbish you eat," my father said. "I hope you'll be able to go in tomorrow."

"I'm alright now," I told him.

"You should not have been rolling down that hill today. It'll make you light in the head," my mother said as she took off her coat and put on her apron before going into the kitchen. "Get to bed early tonight and you'll be alright tomorrow," she predicted.

"Did you have anything to eat yet?" my mother asked my father.

"I have a bit of coddle on," he replied, as he picked up the paper and sat in the chair beside the kitchen table to have a read before supper.

So I now knew what year it was, but still could not begin to understand how I got here. I was a fifteen-year-old youth with the mind of a mature adult and if I had indeed come back in time, I knew what the future held. After a plate of coddle, which was eaten in the kitchen that also doubled as mine and my brother's bedroom, I decided to go into the front room to watch TV before going to bed – but I was stopped in my tracks. We had no TV. Back then we hadn't even got electricity. The rooms were lit by gas mantles, which were mounted on a bracket on the sidewall of each room, one gaslight in each room and the light was quite good from them. Cooking was carried out on a four-ring black cast iron gas stove with a large oven, paid for by inserting pennies into a meter. Water was obtained for cooking, drinking and washing from a large white sink unit, on the landing between the second and third floor, which dispensed cold water and was shared by the other tenants in the house. The toilet, or lavo as we called it, was a concrete shed with a toilet pot in the back yard. In the 50s and 60s these were the living conditions of thousands of people who still lived in tenement buildings in the city.

*****

I slept with my brother Joe in a double bed and our parents slept in a double bed in the front room. I remembered when we were children we used to sometimes sing ourselves to sleep, but when Joe, in bed that night, started to sing I did not join him. My mind was still reeling, trying to come to terms with what had happened to me. How had I become a fifteen-year-old boy again?

I lay awake trying to piece together the events of the day, but was unable to do so, when I suddenly remembered that from the window in the back room, which faced south, I could see the Dublin Mountains, and if the night was clear, the humped outline of The Hellfire Club. I remembered how in the life I had just come from I had often stood at Annette's grave in Bohernabreena Cemetery and looked up the hill at The Hellfire Club; remembering how, when I lived in Wellington Street I often gazed out of this very bedroom window – fascinated by the mound of rock on the hill far away across the city skyline.

I got out of bed and pulled back the curtains searching for it now. And there it was. It seemed to be looking back at me, calling me even. The night was particularly clear and the old ruin seemed to be silhouetted against the bright moonlit sky. In a past life, which now seemed to be repeating itself, I had often stood, as I was now, looking towards the mountains and wondering why was I so captivated by this old ruin, by this view. I tried to remember what thoughts I had back then as I gazed across the city, a much smaller city than the one I had just come from, but my mind was unable to resurrect the attraction it held for me then, though I could quite clearly remember doing exactly what I was doing now.

I stood at the window for a long time as all manner of

thoughts and speculation entered my confused mind. *Why did I so often, in a past life, stand and look at this mountain? Did I know even then that it would be a special place for me? In that other life had I any sense of having lived before and was I now repeating it all again? If I went there now would Annette's grave be there? Would both our names be on the headstone? How many timeframes had there been since her passing? Did I die in another one?*

OH MY GOD…Is Annette alive in this timeframe?

As I stood in the darkness of my old bedroom my mind was a volcano of erupting thoughts and theories, but none that needed testing more than this one.

If I was back in 1960, a young boy again, was she out there? A young girl? Was she, at this very moment, living in Newbridge, County Kildare?

My mind was about to explode and within a matter of seconds I was no longer afraid, I no longer cared for answers as to how I had come here. I was consumed now by one question only – *was Annette alive?* I had to find her if she was.

Annette's father Bill was a saw doctor and in 1960 he was working for Sanderson's Cutlery in Newbridge while he and his family lived in Pairc Mhuire. Annette was attending the local convent school and working part time in Kearns' Ice Cream Parlour. I had to know if this was true of this time I now found myself in. The chance to see and be with her again was almost incomprehensible, but if it was at all possible I had to know.

*****

I lay awake all night and as I did I decided to go to Newbridge the very next day – how I would get there though I did not know. I checked my pockets and all my clothes for money, but all were empty – some things it seemed never change, no matter what timeframe it was. Nevermind, I would get money from somewhere, but for now, more importantly, I needed a plan. I tried to remember all the things Annette told me about her time in Newbridge, but unfortunately I could remember little, just where she lived and worked, the names of one or two of her friends and the fact that the family moved to Dublin in 1961or 62 was the best I could do. That was enough though, this was 1960 and if the same conditions prevailed in this timeframe as the one I had just come from then Annette was alive and well and living in Newbridge and I had the opportunity to see and be with her again.

The next morning I was still awake when I heard my father getting up at half six to go to work. He came into the kitchen/bedroom to make a cup of tea and noticed me awake.

"How are you today? Are you going to work?" He wanted to know.

"I don't know, I'll see later," I answered, knowing full well I was not.

"Do you want a cup of tea?" he asked.

"Is there any coffee?" I replied.

"Coffee? Your ma never buys coffee," he answered and looked at me quizzically.

"Ok, tea will have to do so."

"Are you alright?"

"Yeah, why?" I mischievously looked at him and smiled.

"Coffee!" he said and shook his head.

I watched as he filled the large aluminium kettle with water from the white water bucket and put it on the gas ring before lighting the flame with a Maguire & Patterson match. Then with the same match he lit his first Woodbine of the day. I proceeded to watch him as he buttered a piece of bread and my mind was filled with images of his death from Emphysema. I was tempted to ask him to give up the cigarettes, but I knew it would be like asking a fish not to swim. Anyway that's not what I was here for, so I stopped my minds reverie and brought myself back to the present.

"Do you have any money Da?" I heard myself ask.

"Money?" he responded in a surprised tone.

"Yeah," I laugh, "you know, what you buy things with."

He took a drag from his Woodbine looked at me and said, "What's got into you, first coffee and now money? Your ma said you were acting strange in the park yesterday too, and last night, what were you looking for in the front room? You were looking around the place as if something was missing from the room."

"Oh that," I said as nonchalantly as I could, "I was looking for the television."

"The television!" he exclaimed, "sure we've no television."

"Yeah, I know, I forgot." I said and laughed.

He shook his head in disbelief and sighed, as I smiled quietly remembering how it used to be all those years ago and the way it could be now that I had knowledge of the future and knew what was ahead of us. We were never that close da and me, though we did communicate and after I was married we even went for a drink together now and then, but there was always the reserve that was between fathers and sons in that era and I could see now the potential there was for breaking that reserve down and having a better relationship with him this time round. There was an easy silence for a while as we both contemplated the new, almost playful situation we found ourselves in, then the sound of the kettle coming to the boil broke the silence and da continued making the tea. He handed me a cup as I sat up in the bed, being careful not to wake Joe who was still asleep at the opposite end. I could see a smile on da's face and I was hoping he was thinking about our exchange and finding it amusing.

"About the money Da, do you have a few bob to spare that you could lend me 'til I get paid?" I asked and looked pleadingly at him.

This relaxed, almost buddy talk, was all new to both of us and I had no idea what was going through his mind as he searched my face, no doubt trying to figure out this new casual friendliness towards him by his eldest son.

"You weren't in work yesterday and if you don't go in today you won't have any money to pay me back or give your ma her wages, and I'll get an earful from her about it, so I will," he replied.

"Please, Da, it's important, I wouldn't ask you if it wasn't," I said, all joking now cast aside.

"How much do you want?"

"I don't know, what's the bus fare to Newbridge?"

"Newbridge? What's in Newbridge?" he looked puzzled now.

"My future," I told him, hoping he would not want to know what that was.

"What's got into you at all, I never heard you talking like this before. You sound like, like…I don't know what to make of you!" he concluded in exasperation.

Then as we both lapsed back into silence and I thought I had blown it and would have to try to get the bus fare somewhere else, I saw him fumbling in his trouser pocket before throwing some coins onto the bed and saying, "Here, that's all I have, it should be enough to secure your *future*," before putting his coat and cloth cap on and leaving for

14

work.

I grabbed the coins and began counting them, calling after him as he went out the door, "Thanks Da I'll pay you back."

I picked up the coins, coins I had not seen the like of in over fifty years, half crowns, two shilling pieces, six penny pieces and large brown penny coins, enough I was sure to get me to Newbridge and back.

As soon as I was sure my da was gone I got up, waking my brother in the process, and teased him with the news that I was not going to work but he was still going to school. I threw the dregs of tea into the slop basin and reminded myself to get a cup of coffee as soon as I could. Then I began looking in the old chest of drawers for my clothes. I shuddered when I saw what I had to wear, did I really wear these things? I picked out a red v-necked jumper which I remembered wearing and liked, a white shirt (all my shirts were white) a pair of black trousers and tartan socks and a pair of heavy black shoes. By now my mother was awake and in the kitchen asking us what we wanted for our breakfast. The choice was staggering, Snow Cake or Kerry Cream biscuits! I told her I was going to skip breakfast as I had to go somewhere.

"Are you not going to work?" she asked in a surprised tone.

"Not today," I said and stuck my tongue out at Joe.

"You weren't in yesterday either, you're going to lose that job," she reminded me.

"No I won't," I told her as I put the money into my trouser pocket and took my navy lumber jacket off the back of a chair.

As she and my brother watched I added, "I won't be home 'til late this evening Ma."

"Where are you going?"

"To see your daughter-in-law," I called back, as I opened the door and ran down the stairs.

Chapter three

ANNETTE was fourteen when we met again in September 1960. She had been eighteen, almost nineteen, when I met her for the first time in Bray in 1965.

There was forty five years between those meetings, forty five years during which we fell in love, fell out of love, fell in love again, married, raised a family and shared a life.

I knew of Annette Kennedy long before I ever met her for the first time in 1965, but I did not know her personally before we met at the foot of Bray Head on a warm sunny August Bank Holiday Sunday in 1965. My knowledge of her derived from the fact that from 1959 until 1964 I was a member of a youth football club in Dublin.

The Dominican Friars of Dominick Street ran the club and every year some of the lads in the club were taken for a short holiday to the Dominican College in Newbridge, Co. Kildare. I never went on any of those trips, but when they came back some of the lads used to talk about going to an ice cream parlour in the town where the speciality was ice cream and orange juice highballs, served by a good looking young girl, a "fine thing" as some of them related the story. I took little interest in those stories at the time and I had no idea that one day fate would decree that the paths of this "fine thing" and I would cross, resulting in us becoming man and wife and remaining so for over forty years. It was only when we had been going out together for some time and we began to talk about ourselves that I discovered Annette was the young girl who dispensed highballs and bad thoughts to my friends a few years previously.

When I reached Newbridge I went in search of Kearns' ice cream parlour, I had been to the town with Annette in our previous life but by then the shop was long gone and I was not quite sure exactly where it had been. I walked down the main street looking at the names of the many small shops lining the street until, at last, I was standing outside Kearns'. My mind was racing with excitement at the prospect of seeing Annette again and I stood outside the door almost afraid to enter the shop. *What if she was not there? What if she did not exist in this timeframe or whatever this was?*

As I hesitated to enter, the shop door suddenly opened and a woman came out with a little girl eating an ice cream cone and held the door open so that I could enter. I went in and stood just inside the door. I was terrified to look, but as I stood standing at the door my eyes scanned the small cafe. Then I saw her behind the counter. How I kept my composure on seeing her again I'll never know. The last time I laid eyes on her she was in a coffin. That was April 2009, but now as I saw her again, both of us full of youth – full of life, I wanted to go to her, put my arms around her, hold her and tell her how much I loved her and how much I had missed her since she passed out of my life. I wanted time to be forever frozen at this moment.

I walked in and sat at a table before she came over to me, and as she stood over me I said, "Hi, Annette, can I have a highball please?"

She had no idea who I was and she was visibly astonished when this cheeky young Dublin gurrier, a complete stranger to her, used her name.

I kept my composure and sat looking at her as she stood over me, giving me one of the searching looks that I was so familiar with, and I had missed so much.

She took my order without a word and turned away from me to get my highball as my eyes welled up with tears. I tried to smile and my smile turned to tears of joy as I looked at the tallish, slim young girl with auburn shoulder length hair and hazel eyes who looked far too mature for the loose fitting convent school skirt and jumper she was wearing. A huge contrast to the beautiful glamorous woman she would become, the woman who would turn many a man's head, and I would be fortunate enough to love and call my wife.

I turned to look out the window I was sitting beside so as not to let her see me crying. When she came back a few minutes later she had two highballs on a tray. Still, without saying a word she placed one in front of me and pulled a chair and sat down across the table facing me, leaving the other tall glass of ice cream and orange juice on the tray in front of her as she searched my face for a sign of recognition. As we both sat in silence I was transfixed by the apparition in front of me. Then she broke the magical moment.

"How did you know my name?" she asked with all the authority of a much older girl.

"Someone told me."

"What's wrong with you?" She could see my eyes filling with tears.

"I'm just happy to see you…" I almost said "again."

"Why are you happy to see me? You don't know me."

I hesitated as I did not at that moment know how much I should tell her or how much she would be able to understand, after all she was only fourteen in this time and I, myself, at that moment did not fully understand what had happened to me, what had caused me to be here now. I stared at her as she waited for an answer to her question, a girl I had married and had three children with in another time, and all I could say was, "I just am, and I do know you."

"How do you know me?" She persisted. "I've never seen you before, you're not from around here are you?"

I reached across the table, barely letting my fingers touch her hand, which she did not move away, and I said, "I know you as well as I know myself, as well as if we had spent a lifetime together."

She looked at me uneasily and then pulled her hand back from mine, stood up, and holding the other highball on the tray turned away from the table and said, "You're mad."

As she walked back behind the counter she turned and looked at me again with a puzzled expression on her face, as if she was trying to remember if she had in fact seen or met me before. I sat eating and drinking my highball, all the time watching her as she went about her work serving people in the shop, and every now and then glancing over in my direction with a quizzical look on her face. When my highball was finished I remained at the table until it was time for Annette to finish her shift. When I saw her putting on her school coat I got up and stood at the door, opening it for her as she stepped out onto the street where I stood with her.

"Where are you going?" She asked as we stood outside the shop.

"I'll walk you home," I said. "Pairc Mhuire, that's where you live isn't it?"

"How did you know that?" she asked, surprised by my knowledge.

"I told you, I know all about you," I said with a smile.

"You can't come home with me," she exclaimed, a look of worry on her face now.

"Mary and Bill won't mind, they like me" I replied and smiled as I stood beside her suppressing a strong desire to take her in my arms and kiss her.

"How did you know…?" she almost screamed in surprise.

"I told you," I interjected and led her away from the shop door by the arm. "Look," I said as we walked down the street, all the time Annette looking at me with a silent curiosity and certain wariness. "I have to catch my bus back to Dublin shortly so I don't have the time to explain myself now. I'll walk you home, but can I come back to see you again at the weekend?"

She did not reply to my question but just continued to walk beside me down the street as if in a trance. I walked beside her and took her hand, which she did not resist, and all the time it seemed she was trying hard to understand what was happening. We walked the short distance from the shop to Pairc Mhuire in silence.

I don't know what was going through Annette's mind but I was in a state of total bliss, this was something I had thought would never happen again, but here I was, walking with my wife and holding her hand, and she was alive! I had thought that this was impossible after what I knew had happened in the last two years. I led her up the street and surprised her when I turned down the lane, which leads to Pairc Mhuire from the main street. She released my hand and stood at the corner of the lane deep, in thought as I waited for her to follow me.

Then she said, "I told you, you can't come home with me."

I walked back to her and again took her hand in mine before saying, "There's a lot I don't understand either Annette, but I want to see you again and maybe I'll be able to explain things a bit better then."

As we both contemplated this strange encounter there

21

was nothing more I could say at that moment in time that would go anywhere near explaining my presence in her life, five years before the time we had met in another timeframe. All I knew was that I was elated to be with her again, with the prospect of having those five extra years with her.

I had no idea what had happened to me so how I was going to explain that to a fourteen-year-old schoolgirl was beyond my comprehension. *How was I going to tell her that we were once married and had raised a family in another life and that I had somehow, it seemed, crossed the barriers of time to be with her again? And what consequences, if any, would that have for our future as I remembered it?* At that moment I did not care, I had got what I had been wishing and praying for since Annette passed away, the chance to live our lives all over again.

In that other time our first kiss had not occurred until our third date on the corner of Le Fanu Road in Ballyfermot, but as I left Annette outside her house in Pairc Mhuire, having only just met her again, I was not stricken with the youthful shyness of my past life and I gently kissed her on the cheek, savouring the touch and smell of her skin once more.

As I walked briskly away over the small patch of grass outside her house to the narrow lane which would bring me back to the main street of the sleepy country town to catch my bus back to Dublin I turned my head and Annette was still standing outside her house looking after me, and touching her hand to the side of her face that I had kissed.

I was buzzing with excitement and anticipation at what was going to happen next, now that we were together again.

Chapter four

SITTING on the old cream and brown coloured CIE bus, on my way back to Dublin, my mind returned to the still so very confusing and frightening events, which had caused me to travel to Newbridge to test my assumptions and discover if the seemingly impossible had really happened – and I had taken a trip through time.

I was now, after seeing Annette, convinced I had. I really had travelled back through time, but I now had to try to figure out how this situation had arisen.

How was I once again a fifteen-year-old boy with the knowledge of having lived another life in another time, and with the intelligence and intellect of someone much older than fifteen?

How could I begin to explain all this to a fourteen-year-old schoolgirl without her thinking I was some kind of weirdo peddling stories for some perverse reason, when I didn't at that moment have a clue how it had happened myself? How could I tell this young girl I had only just met that one day she would marry me and give birth to three children?

Knowing the Annette of the last timeframe, as I did, and if this Annette was in the least bit similar, I knew that if I told her that, that is exactly what she would endeavour not to do.

On the more than two-hour long bumpy journey back to Dublin, which took less than an hour in another time on a motorway not yet built, I tried to convince myself that I would think of something that would make sense of the situation I found myself in – something that would make sense to both of us. After all if I could travel through time surely I could figure that out.

I was now two days back in this timeframe, experiencing things I had not done or experienced in my other existence. *Or was it the same one, the same existence, the only difference being I had knowledge of the future? Would things turn out completely different this time? Would this Annette be a completely different person to the girl I fell in love with and married in another life?*

I hoped not.

*****

It was almost 8pm by the time I got home after seeing Annette that Wednesday, and as I made my way up O'Connell Street I was amused and delighted to see buskers once more providing great entertainment singing and playing musical instruments while working the queues of people at the cinemas. This was something I had forgotten ever existed in Dublin.

With the option to pre-book in the time I had come from, there was seldom a need to queue, thus eliminating this source of income for buskers.

The Metropole looked fantastic with its huge canopy, which stretched almost to the end of the footpath advertising *Doctors In Love* as the featured film attraction, and the great Peggy Dell as provider of entertainment in the Georgian Supper Room. The Capitol was showing *Five Branded Women* starring Silvana Mangano, and with its front illuminated with multicoloured neon lights and the marble steps leading to a well-lit foyer it looked so inviting. Those marvellous old cinemas should never have been knocked down, they were works of art.

Further up the street the Savoy and Carlton were doing a brisk business showing *Anna Of Brooklyn* and *Confessions Of A Counter Spy*. Facing on up the street a huge billboard over the canopy of The Ambassador was advertising *Ben Hur*. Nelson was standing in all his majesty, towering over a much grander and impressive thoroughfare than the tacky, rundown and junkie-infested street I remembered from 2010.

The old, very tall, speckled grey columned streetlights looked almost balletic as they stood casting their light from two outstretched wing-like arms on the very many green double-decker buses, and the, to me, almost vintage cars moving up and down the street – and indeed parked in the middle of the street.

At the beginning of the street near O'Connell Bridge, was the Green Rooster Restaurant, and when I saw it my memory went into overdrive as I stood looking at the outline of the multicoloured stained glass rooster, which dominated the front window. I was remembering shortly after we married the last time around and moved into our house in Clinches Court on the North Strand, how after a late Saturday night of dancing we used to spend the morning in bed and then head into town for lunch, very often in the Green Rooster. I almost cried with joy at the prospect of doing it all again. After Annette went out of my life I had wished and prayed so fervently to be given another chance at the life we had shared and as I stood at the window of the Green Rooster, now back in 1960 again, it seemed like my prayers had been answered.

I continued on up O'Connell Street, taking in all the sounds of a past age and deriving great pleasure from seeing the grandeur of all the old buildings I had forgotten about. The elephant was again over the door of what used to be Elverys sports shop on the corner of O'Connell Street and Abbey Street. It now housed the offices of the new *Evening Press* newspaper, with its big street front windows full of pictures of glamorous people enjoying the social events of the day. In 2010, where I had been just a few days ago, this building was a fast food restaurant. The Victorian Bar in Princes Street next to the Capitol was there again, as was Murphy's jewellers on the corner of the Metropole building where I had bought a Celtic necklace for Annette's 21st birthday, with the money I had got from the sale for my collection of Frank Sinatra records back in a 1967 of another time line. Further on up the street was the very imposing building housing Gills religious art and publishing business, which in the time I had come from was just a hole in the ground hidden by a hording.

The past was alive again. Passing the throngs of happy people on the street on their way to a night out in one of the many cinemas in the city centre the thought crossed my mind that very many of them were probably dead in the time I had just come from. I may even have been at one or two of the funerals! Is this, I thought, what eternal life means, we just keep repeating our lives all over again? I crossed the road at the corner of Frederick Street and Dorset Street and to my right was 'The Red Brick College' my old school, St. Joseph's Boys' National School, Dorset Street. In 2010 the old red-bricked building was part of The Mater Hospital. I passed Connolly's vegetable shop and Norton's grocery shop, where my mother had done most of her shopping in the 50s and early 60s, before the advent of supermarkets, and then I turned into Wellington Street.

The old street was buzzing with life. No one had televisions then and only a few had radios. Computers, PlayStations, iPods and DVDs had not even begun to be figments of our imaginations at that time. All our amusement and entertainment was attained on the street or in the Plaza Cinema just down the road.

This was the first time, since I was back in this era, that I had seen any of my contemporaries from my last life. Cullens' little sweet shop was still open and as usual Joe Evans was in there, chasing Mary Cullen the shop assistant. At the wall of Glennons' fuel and vegetable shop on the corner of the butter factory lane, across from the "Dairo," which was Kennedy's Bakery yard, Spud Murphy and Foxie Fox were playing handball. Mick Lawless and Pat Murray were sitting talking to Christine Campbell and Maria O'Leary on the steps of Mick's house. Sissie McDonald, Joe Cahill and six or seven others were playing rounder's in the middle of the street. There were very few cars, I remembered that from before, and none at all in Wellington Street, so the street belonged to the children. Various other kids, including my younger brother Joe, were playing marbles against the pavement kerb. All this activity was going on under the watchful eyes of women looking out of the open windows of the tall tenement buildings, which lined both sides of the street from the "Dairo" lane up to Mountjoy Street. Amongst the women with their heads out the windows was my mother.

As I walked up the street Mick Lawless saw me and called over to me, "Are you coming out Andrew?"

At the same time my mother saw me and called from the window, "Where in the name of God were you 'til this hour?"

Mick answered for me and laughed, "He was with his

"moth." I ignored him and shouted up to my mother that I'd be up in a minute before going over to Mick, Pat, Christine and Maria. It had been so long since I had last seen them that I had almost forgotten what they looked like, and that I had lived a lifetime since we had all been together like this before. I started to babble to them with great excitement like I had not seen them in years, which indeed I hadn't, forgetting that, in their minds, they had probably seen and spoken to me only a few days ago. I also forgot that I was speaking as a mature man while they were still adolescents.

"How are you all?" I gushed excitedly. "What have you been doing with your lives, it's great to see you all again!"

They looked at me in astonishment and then at each other, but did not say anything. Then I realised where I was and laughed and said, "Only joking, I'll be down when I get my dinner, wait here for me and we'll have a game of rounders or go for a ramble."

I then ran over to number fifty five, pushed in the heavy wooden door and ran up the six flights of stairs to the third floor where my parents were alive and well again.

Chapter five

I WENT to work in Burroughs & Watts the next day, hoping that I would be able to remember how to tip a cue and stitch the cloth of a billiard table. I hoped also that my workmates would not notice any difference in me or my attitude. I left the house that morning and ran down the six flights of stairs feeling exhilarated at the prospect of seeing Annette again at the weekend. I pulled open the hall door of the old tenement and stepped once more into 1960.

Joan Dempsey was standing at the door of her little grocery shop across the street, having just opened for another day's trading. Joan ran the shop with her partner Tony. I waved to her and walked down the street towards the Dairo lane at the side of the bakery, passing Stanley's pig yard as I went, and inhaled once more the pungent smell of pig slop. I stopped for a moment and looked at the old square of small whitewashed houses in Paradise Place then went past St Mary's Christian Brothers School and the Plaza Cinema, down Dorset Street and into Dominick Street where I knew I would soon be living in the new flats that were nearing completion. I crossed Parnell Street and proceeded down Chapel Lane, which led me to the back entrance of Burroughs & Watts. My aunt Maggie worked in the cardboard box factory, which was next door to B&W, it was she who got me the job there after I left school in 1959 at the age of fourteen. I could not wait to get out of school, I hated it and there was never any chance of me furthering my education in secondary school. I hated classroom learning, so any more learning or education for me would be in the wide-open spaces of the school of life.

Before sliding open the green gate to gain access to my work place I looked in through the open door of the box factory and there standing at her machine stapling boxes was Maggie. I raised my hand in greeting to her and over the noise of the machine she mouthed back, "Are you better?" I nodded my head in reply and a tear came to my eyes at seeing her again, she died when I was about nineteen in my last life.

When I went into work Tom Coulter, Liam Stephens and Christy Manning were already in. Tom was having a cup of tea before starting his day's work and Liam was poring over the racing pages of *The Daily Express* while Christy was singing as he loaded his van with stock for another trip out of town. As "junior partner" it was my job to make a cup of tea each morning before we started work, but obviously they thought I was not coming in to day so someone else had made the brew. I shouted a cheery good morning to them, and Liam, raising his head from his paper jokingly said, "Ah the production manager is back. (The production manager was his nickname for me because I was always telling him how he could get the work done quicker) Enjoy your tea lads we'll be drinking piss again tomorrow."

It was so strange seeing my old workmates from the time I was just a youth in another life and me having lived a whole lifetime since then. I knew Christy had passed away in the 1980s of that other life and I was pretty sure Tom Coulter would have been dead in that time too as he was well into his 60s now. I lost contact with Liam, but it was possible that he would have been still alive in the time I had come from as he was not many years older than me. I really enjoyed my two years in Burroughs & Watts, it was so easy going and they were a great crowd to work with.

Tom, the senior of the crew, asked me if I was better as my aunt Maggie had told him I was not well. I told him I was fine again and ready for work so he handed me a list of clients who were waiting for a service call from me. After a quick cup of tea I gathered my gear, cue tips, glue discs, chalk, table markers, needles and green thread, and my piece of 1960s "advanced technology," an Andrew's Liver Salt can with a hole in it to allow a jet of hot steam escape from the boiled water in the can to melt the glue discs to tip the cues. I put everything into my little wooded case and went out into "Dublin In The Rare Oul Times," once more.

I went through the next few days as if I was walking on a cloud, even the feigned gruffness of my boss, Tom Bennett could not upset me as I went about my work servicing the pool tables of Dublin's finest gentlemen's clubs – The United Services Club, The Stephen's Green Club, The Friendly Brothers Club, The College of Surgeons and The Mount Street Gentlemen's Club amongst them. I took great pleasure and delight in seeing Dublin in its pre-boom time again. The imposing edifice of The Theatre Royal was still standing proudly in Hawkins Street beside the less imposing, but still sadly missed, Regal Rooms cinema.

The old green CIE buses were running down Grafton Street sharing the street with their colleagues from the freight section of CIE on their large wooden flat-bottomed carts from which they collected and delivered goods to the businesses in the city. These carts were pulled by sturdy horses, and there were lots of pushbikes everywhere too. A Garda, in his gleaming white jacket and gloves was directing traffic from his box on a flower bedecked O'Connell Bridge. Seemingly always in good humour as he shared a word and a joke with the pedestrians, as they passed in safety under his box.

The lady with the long flowing grey hair was playing her harp on Wicklow Street, and the news boys, as they shouted, *Herald, Mail or Press* brought back all kinds of memories to me. The Guinness barges on the Liffey were a joy to behold as they sailed, piled high with barrels of Guinness from the brewery at Ushers Island to the Lady Grania and the Lady Gwendolen, the two blue and cream Guinness ships with the red funnel's which were docked beside the Custom House and carried the precious cargo to England. The old low-slung barges had to lower their funnels passing under the bridges when the tide was high, and the sight of them meandering lazily up and down the river reminded me that I must take a trip across it on the, long gone in the time I had come from, Liffey Ferries. All this nostalgia was reinforced for me by the sense of safety and good humour and a lack of unfortunate beggars and junkies on the streets, which was so much a part of the city I had just come from. It made me sad to realise just how much of Dublin's old character and charm, had been lost in the name of progress in the time I had come from.

Against the backdrop of Molly's fair city becoming alive for me again I merged into the fabric of the old place and lost myself in its charm. That night I did, in fact, take a trip across the river on the ferry, paying six pence for the privilege. As the ferry boat "chuck, chuck, chucked" its way across the dark brown Liffey swell near, what in the time I had come from was the O2 concert venue, I stood in the little boat with six or seven others, mostly dock workers, and looked up the still working quays devoid of bridges until Butt Bridge. There were lots of ships tied against the quay walls and the tall cranes used to load and unload them were moving up and down the tracks on the road near the river. All this activity was carried on against a backdrop of buildings, warehouses and a huge grey circular gas tank whose space would, years later, be occupied by tall office blocks rendering most of this river skyline gone. It was a marvellous time to be young again I thought to myself as I stood like Admiral Nelson himself in the little ferry crossing the river. But this time, I vowed, I was going to appreciate it so much more that I had done the last time.

I went to work again the next morning with a spring in my step after my boat trip, and knowing that I would be going to Newbridge again the following day, I could not wait for the day to end. I did not go out with my friends as I usually did on Friday nights, but stayed in and washed myself in the old tin washbasin, which substituted for a bath in the tenements.

First thing Saturday morning I got up and looked for my best clothes, which turned out to be the red jumper and white shirt I had worn on Wednesday. I reluctantly put them on and promised myself a trip to Power and Moore's in Talbot Street, as soon as I could, to replenish my wardrobe. I told my mother that I would be out all day and not to make any dinner for me before running down the stairs lest she quiz me about where I was going. I walked briskly down an almost deserted O'Connell Street to Bus Aras to catch the early bus to Newbridge.

Chapter six

ALL I had said to Annette before I left her on Wednesday was that I would see her at the weekend, giving her no hint of the day or time I would arrive. When I got off the bus in Newbridge it was after 1.30pm so I made my way straight to Kearns' Ice Cream Parlour and looked in the window. Annette was there, but she was not working. She was sitting at a table smoking a cigarette and having a mineral with a boy about my own age. Her hair was piled high on her head and she was wearing a red jumper and cream coloured skirt. He was wearing a blue and red check shirt and a pair of badly cut jeans with large turn-ups, over a pair of brown sandals, with black stockings .

It was so strange seeing Annette smoking again. She was never a heavy smoker, a packet of twenty Players would last her almost the week, but still the sight of her smoking was a bit strange. She had given up cigarettes in the early 80s and I had almost forgotten she had ever smoked. I don't know what surprised me more, seeing her smoking again or being with a boy. She did not see me so I just watched them for a few minutes. They seemed quite relaxed with each other and were laughing and talking. The boy, although I was sure I did not know him, looked vaguely familiar to me. As I continued looking at them through the window they suddenly stood up and Annette put her cigarettes and matches into a small black hand bag and the boy helped her put her coat on, which was her school coat, and then held Annette's hand as they headed for the door. I remained where I was at the window as they came out of the shop and when they were outside I took a step towards them, smiled at Annette and said,

"Hello, Annette, I told you I'd be back at the weekend, and here I am." She looked surprised to see me and the boy looked at her and then at me. "Who are you?" he asked in a thick Kildare accent. I deliberately ignored him and said to Annette,

"Annette we have a lot to talk about, I've come a long way to see you and I'd like to talk to you alone."

For one of the few times since I'd known her, Annette seemed lost for words and she just stood looking at me in silence. The boy, sensing the tension in Annette, looked at me and raising his voice said, "I said who the fuck are you?" and letting go of Annette's hand he stuck his face into mine. I held my ground still ignoring him and looked intently at Annette before saying, "My name is Andy Halpin." I was hoping against hope that the name would awaken a spark of recognition somewhere in the deep recesses of Annette's mind, if it was possible to "remember" your future.

But I could see my name meant nothing to her. The boy then turned to Annette and said, "Do you know him?"

"No," she replied as I held her gaze.

"Then how does he know you?" he demanded.

"He was in the shop on Wednesday," she told him, "and he says he knows me, but I never saw him before in my life."

Not in this life I thought, but you knew me very well in another. I now had a dilemma, it seemed Annette and this boy were boyfriend and girlfriend and I certainly did not want to land her in trouble with him so I had to think quickly.

"I know Annette through friends of mine," I said. "I'm a member of a football club and some of the lads from the team came to Newbridge on holidays. They told me Annette makes great orange and ice cream highballs. My father owns a cafe in Dublin and the lads wanted us to make highballs the same way Annette does, so I want her to teach me how she makes them so I'll be able to make them the same way in our café." I lied.

The boy looked at Annette, then at me and said incredulously, "You came all the way from Dublin just for that?"

"Yes," I said. "We like to keep our customers happy." I held my ground as he looked me up and down. I then sneaked a glance at Annette and I could see her looking at me suspiciously. I knew that look so well. Whenever I was trying to pull something over on her she'd give me a look that, without a word being spoken, said, "Do you think I'm a complete fool?"

The boy then laughed and said to Annette, "Jayus, you better tell him how to make them highballs so and let him get back to Dublin."

He then kissed Annette on the lips and said, "I have to get back to practice now, I'll see you tonight," and to me, "Good luck with your highballs."

He then walked down the street leaving me and Annette standing on the footpath outside Kearns' shop. We said nothing until he was gone and then Annette looked at me and spoke. "Do you think I'm a complete fool, who are you and what do you want? How did you know who I was, and don't give me anything about the boys from the football club and highballs, I know that's a pack of lies."

It was time to be honest, as hard as this was going to be

I decided not to waste time prevaricating. I did not know how much time I was going to be here, I could be whisked back to 2010 at any moment, so I was going to tell Annette the truth as far as I knew it.

"I have to get the five o'clock bus back to Dublin," I said. "So we don't have a lot of time for me to explain what I'm going to tell you. Would you like to go back into the cafe so we can sit down while we talk?"

"No," she said. "I'd prefer to go someplace else, there's a little cake shop down the road, we can go there."

"OK, lead the way."

We walked in silence for about two or three minutes until we came to a tearooms with cakes in the window, pink and whites, snow cakes, gur cakes and fresh cream scones – cakes I had not seen in years. We went in and found a table at the end of the long narrow tearoom. As we waited to be served Annette took off her coat and put it across the back of an empty chair at the table, took her cigarettes and matches from her bag and sat down. She offered me a cigarette, which I refused, and she lit one herself. As she inhaled and blew the smoke across the table she looked so much older than her fourteen years. The waitress who came to serve us was a friend of Annette's, Ann Devlin, whom I remembered Annette speaking about in a past lifetime. She took our order for tea and snow cakes and as she did so she looked at me and said to Annette, "How's Willie?" who I presumed was the boy who had been with her earlier. When Ann went to get our order I said to Annette, "I hope I didn't get you into trouble with Willie."

"Why would you get me into trouble with Willie?" she asked.

"Well he might think…"

"He has no reason to be thinking anything," she said,

interrupting me. When Ann brought us the tea and cakes she stood at the table as if waiting for Annette to introduce her to me, but Annette just stubbed out her cigarette and smiled a very un-fourteen-year-old-like smile and said, "That's grand Ann, thank you."

And then in a manner I was so familiar with, she turned back to me, looked me straight in the eyes and said, " Well?"

Here goes I thought, *I better make this good. I've a feeling I'll only get one chance at it.*

"Annette" I said, " last Wednesday when I told you that I knew you as if we'd spent a lifetime together I was telling the truth. I do know you and we have spent a lifetime together. Not this lifetime but in another timeframe when we were married, when we were husband and wife. In that other time I met you at the foot of Bray Head when you were eighteen years old. It was August, Sunday 1965. We married three years later and raised a family. We had three children, David, Gina and Robert and three grandchildren, Senan, Ella May and Mina. We lived for over thirty years in Tallaght and after…"

I hesitated there and decided not to say anything about her passing.

"In 2010 something happened to me, something I can't explain, but it caused me to travel back through time, to this year, 1960, five years before we met in another time. I could not resist the chance it gave me to see you and spend that extra time with you… so here I am!" I stopped speaking and waited for a response from Annette who had sat listening to my story in silence and after what seemed like a period of profound reflection on her part she looked straight into my eyes once more and said, "That's just not possible, people can't travel through time, that's a load of lies. That kind of thing only happens in films."

I saw an opening in that statement and said, "You can do anything in the movies" and hoped against hope that somehow, somewhere in the depths of her subconscious, that would register with her as a remark I used many a time in our last life when she questioned the practicality of something I wanted to do. But I was grasping at straws and it was obvious that it meant nothing to her.

She stubbed out the cigarette and stood up and reached for her coat. I grabbed her arm and holding it firmly said, "Please Annette, don't go, what I've told you is the truth. I have travelled through time, I'll prove it to you. I know your mother and father's names and I know you have a brother and four sisters."

"I only have two sisters," she quickly retorted as I continued holding her arm.

"Yes, at the moment you only have two sisters, Marie, and Claire, but you will have two more, Caroline and Louise."

I released her arm and as she continued to stand at the table I said, "Your mother's maiden name is Iveagh spelled I-v-e-a-g-h and you have an uncle Jamesie who lives with your granny Iveagh in Crumlin, on Kildare Road, where you were born and used to live when you were younger. You also have aunts Rosie and Hannah. In the next year or so you will move back to Dublin and live for a while with your aunt Hannah and her family in Ballyfermot before moving into a house of your own on Le Fanu Road in Ballyfermot. You were living there when I met you in 1965."

I stopped talking suddenly as I could see she was getting upset by what I was saying and that was the last thing I wanted to do. I reached for her hand and held it before saying, in as comforting a way as I could, "Please sit down Annette, I don't want to upset you. I've told you I don't know how this thing happened, but we had such a great life

39

together that when I found myself back in this time, and knowing I was destined to meet you in 1965 anyway I could not resist the opportunity to come and see you."

She sat back at the table and I continued holding her hand as I said, "I don't know if I've done right or wrong by telling you about your family, and meeting you sooner than we should have met, but right or wrong I've done it now."

Annette was distressed by what I'd told her and again asked how I knew so much about her and her family, which was only to be expected.

"Who told you about my family, my granny and my aunts?" she asked.

"You did, when we were together in another time. Please believe me Annette the last thing I want to do is upset you. I hated doing that before and I don't want to do it now, but what I'm telling you is the truth, I have travelled back through time."

She looked intently at me and I could feel her squeezing my hand as she said, "It's not true, what you're saying is not true. People can't travel through time, someone told you all about my family… it's not true, I was never married to you. I'm fourteen for God's sake!"

She got up again from the table and started to walk away, but I called after her, "It is true, believe me Annette. You told me all I have just said about you and your family…"

As she continued to walk away from me I walked after her and added, "There's one more thing I know about you Annette, you have two moles on your left shoulder and one on your stomach."

She stopped walking, stood still for a moment and even though she had her back to me, I could almost see the look of panic I knew was on her face. Then she turned to face me and coldly asked, "How do you know that?"

"I told you Annette, we've met before, we've been married in another time."

We stood then, looking into each other's eyes in the middle of the little tearooms as Ann Devlin stood transfixed, looking at us while taking an order from a customer. I took her hand and led her back to the table and we sat down once more. We remained silent for a while as I pondered whether what I had just made was a terrible mistake and then Annette, who had seemed to be reflecting on what I had told her, spoke.

"What you have said is just not possible. It can't be possible for someone to travel back through time."

And then somewhat thoughtfully, as if she was reading my mind, added, "And even if what you are saying is true, which it can't be, then you should not have interfered with events that have not happened yet."

Exactly what I would have expected the Annette of 1965 to say.

"Do you believe me then? That what I'm saying is true, that we have…"

"No, I mean, I don't know…it's not possible," she interjected.

"But I've given you proof. How else would I know all the things I've just told you if you had not told me in another time, in the life we shared as husband and wife?" I pleaded.

"You're confusing me." She was becoming distressed again. "If what you're telling me is true where does my freedom of choice and free will come in? If you know all that is going to happen to me where does that leave me, it means I have no free will."

"I only know what is going to happen to us from August 1965, not what is going to happen to us before then," I said, trying to rationalise, as if this concession made any real difference.

"I never knew you at this time in the past life, this is all new to me too. In that other time I had no idea Annette Kennedy even existed at this point," I told her. "I have no idea what is going to happen to us between now and August 1965."

"I'm frightened," she said. "You know so much about me and I know nothing about you. I don't even know if you are who you say you are."

"I am who I say I am. I'm Andy Halpin. In another time you meet me in 1965 and in 1968 we get married… Only something has happened that has caused me to be in your life again, but five years early," I said, trying to be as calm and unemotional as possible so as not to frighten her even further.

"You should not have come here. You should have let things happen if they were meant to happen. If you are so sure that what you are saying is true you should not have interfered – there's a time for everything," she said, sounding exactly like the intelligent, mature woman I remembered and loved.

"Annette, I loved you so much in our other life that I wanted to be with you as soon as I realised what had happened, and I knew where you were. I knew because you told me you lived in Newbridge in 1960 and worked in Kearns' after school. How else would I have known that" I said as I looked at her and waited for a response.

"I don't love you, I don't know you," is all she said. "You will, I promise you, you will and we'll be very happy."

"And what about Willie?" she asked, puzzling me with her question.

"Who?" I responded, not understanding at first.

"Willie, you just met him, my boyfriend Willie Rogers,

what will happen to him?"

I was flabbergasted, in all the time I'd known Annette she never once mentioned she used to be Willie Rogers' girlfriend. Willie was a huge singing personality in the time I had come from and Annette had never once said she used to be his girlfriend. It was news to me.

"Willie Rogers, is he Willie Rogers?" I asked in disbelief, and then," Don't worry about Willie he'll do alright for himself."

Annette looked at me with a look that belied her young age and said, "I don't know what to make of you. You walk into my life and tell me I was married to you in another time, you know things you should not know about me and my family, things that have not even happened yet, or so you say… but what do you want me to do now, just drop everything and walk away with you?

Now it was my turn to be confused, what *did* I want? To start the relationship now or wait until 1965 came around again?

"No," I said, "I don't want you to walk away with me now, I just wanted to see you. If we start the relationship now I don't know how that will affect our later relationship after 1965. Obviously we will not be meeting for the first time in 1965 now, by meeting you now I have changed that."

"You should not have come here, things only happen when they are meant to happen."

"Annette," I said, "when I found myself back in 1960 I had not… "I stopped myself saying I had not seen her in over a year, knowing if I said that she would ask why, and I did not want to say anything about her passing away in 2009 just yet. What I had told her already was more than enough to be going on with, so I thought for a moment before saying,

"Well I just had not got the willpower to stop myself from

seeing what you were like before I met you."

"And what am I like?"

"A lot like you were back in another time, a strong woman not afraid to speak your mind, someone who makes her own decisions," I told her.

She stood up from the table for the last time then and said, "There's something about you, I don't know what it is, but you seem to believe what you're saying, and if it's true then I should not even be talking to you now. I don't think you should be interfering in something like this, you should let things take their own course, and if we meet again in 1965, well, we'll take it from there."

"Maybe you're right" I agreed, "maybe I should not have come to see you. I hope I have not done anything to cause our future to be any different from the way I remember it."

"Was it that good?" Annette asked.

"It was," I replied before standing up, kissing her tenderly on the lips and walking away – leaving her standing at the table as Ann Devlin looked on, open-mouthed.

I stood outside the door of the teashop wondering what I would do next, this encounter had not turned out the way my foolish imagination had hoped it would. *Had I messed everything up by making myself known to Annette at this time instead of waiting till 1965 to meet her?* I walked slowly up the street in the direction of the bus stop, aware that I was much too early for the bus, but not knowing what else to do now. As I walked up the street, however, I heard Annette call. I turned around and she was walking towards me.

"Wait," she said, "do you want to go for a walk along the river? Your bus won't be in yet…"

*****

Did I want to go for a walk with my wife? Did I want to win the Lotto? I felt like running to her and enveloping her in my arms. I never thought in my wildest dreams that I would ever hear my wife ask me if I wanted to go for a walk again. I just stood looking at her as she began walking towards me and all at once I could see the Annette I'd known and loved again, and hoped I would not be overcome with emotion at what was happening. I waited for her to catch up with me and we walked towards the river near the Dominican College. The day was fine and sunny so we strolled beside the water for a while before sitting on the grass near the water's edge. Annette seemed more relaxed now and as I lay on my back in the grass feeling the warm sun on my face and her gaze scrutinising me I said, "Do you believe me then? That we knew each other before?"

"I don't know, you seem to believe it, but things like that can't happen."

"Unless it's for a purpose" I said, and waited for a response.

"Like what?" Annette asked.

I raised myself up on my elbows and shook my head, I had no answer that would make any sense of the situation we found ourselves in.

"What's it like in 2010?" Annette then asked. "Are things much different?"

I had to think before answering that question. She seemed genuinely interested and if that was the case then she might be beginning to believe me, but still I knew I could not go and tell her everything just yet. I had to get to know this Annette better first.

"People are not a lot different from now, a bit more modern and materialistic and everyone wants to win the Lotto, which is a weekly numbers game for millions of… pounds." I hesitated, not wanting to have to explain Euros, which was even hard to do in 2010.

"Most people have cars, and computers are in almost every home. There is what is called multiplex cinemas, that means instead of a building housing one cinema screen there could be up to ten or twelve cinemas in a single building – exciting or what?" I exclaimed as I tried feebly to entertain her.

"There's also a thing called the Internet that allows you to communicate with people all over the world instantly, and you can download – that means you can get any information on almost anything – from your computer, films and music and such like."

"That sounds like a great world. Have we…I mean have you got a computer?" she asked sheepishly.

"Yes, we have."

"And can I use the computer and get stuff from…what did you call it, a net or something?"

I just looked at her and smiled as I tried to satisfy her curiosity.

"Yes, you can use the computer, you can use it better than I can. You can even shop on the Internet from your own room for all the things you need or want and they are the delivered to you. You also have a phone that you carry around with you all the time, a mobile phone it's called. If you like I'll give you your number and you can try ringing it sometime and have a chat with yourself," I smiled "You can also send what is called text messages on it if you don't feel like talking…"

I could see how interested she was and took heart from that.

"We don't even have a phone in our house here," she responded. "If I wanted to make that phone call to myself I'd have to go to a pub or the phone box down the main street, but there's nearly always somebody in it."

"Everyone has a mobile phone which they carry everywhere they go in 2010," I said. "Phone boxes are almost a thing of the past there."

"What else is there?"

"We are in a thing called the EU, The European Union, and Ireland is a multicultural country, with lots of what are called "New Irish" all over the place. Nothing closes, the radio and the TV stations run programmes all night, and there are loads of different television channels on which all programmes are in colour. Shops and pubs stay open late, some for 24 hours, and politicians are corrupt – otherwise things are much the same."

She seemed genuinely amazed at what I was saying before her mood got a bit more serious and she asked, "And us, what are we like in 2010?"

I did not want to go there. I did not want to talk about our situation just yet, it was too soon. I wanted to get to know this Annette better before I went down that road, though I knew even then that I would have to confront that situation at some point – but not right now.

"Oh, I'm retired" I told her, "I'm an old man back there." I laughed adding, "and you, well I don't think I should say too much about that. You haven't lived it yet and maybe I've said and done enough already."

Thankfully she did not press me on it, so I quickly changed the subject, asking her how long she was going out with Willie Rogers.

"I got to know him through his cousin Eileen. She's in the same class as me and we just started to talk and liked each other's company, that's all really. He wants to be a musician, a singer, he writes songs and I help him with them sometimes, with the words."

"Do you write songs yourself?"

"I try, but I don't think they're any good."

"I bet they're very good," I smile. "Maybe you'll let me hear them sometime…"

It was so easy to talk to Annette. It was as if we had never been apart and I was reluctant to go when it came time for me to catch the bus back to Dublin. Before leaving she made me promise that I would not contact her again, and if we met in 1965, well, we would take things from there. I suppose it was really as much as I could have expected, and maybe more than I deserved for the distress I had caused her.

She walked to the bus stop with me and before boarding I took her in my arms and kissed her, an action she did not resist my doing. She stood on the kerb waving as the bus pulled away from the stop.

I had promised her I would not contact her again until 1965. I just hoped I was strong enough to keep my promise.

Chapter seven

I WAS a fifteen-year-old boy trapped in 1960 with the knowledge of all that was yet to come, and the advantage that knowledge gave me, but the only thing on my mind was Annette and a yearning to be with her. To rekindle, or indeed to kindle for the first time, the love I was missing so much. I knew where she was and was tempted every day to break my promise to her and go to Kildare, but inside the body of the teenager I appeared to be to all the world, was the mind of a mature man, and that wiser counsel told me that, intelligent and all as Annette was, this was not a situation she was finding easy to understand or handle, and I did not want to exert any undue pressure on her.

She had to live the five years until 1965, her formative years, before meeting me, and her mental maturity had to develop before we would or could have the loving relationship we had before. Although I had got what I had been wishing and praying for since Annette passed away in 2009, the way it had come about did not seem like the answer to my prayers or the way I imagined it would be. I was now not so sure that making myself known to Annette at this time was a good idea. I could so easily have jeopardized our future.

I was tormented by these thoughts as I went about my life again in 1960 and I came to the conclusion that if I did impose myself on Annette's life now it would destroy whatever chance we would have of leading the life I remembered. So I decided I would do my best to keep my promise and not go back to Newbridge again, hard and all as I knew that would be.

From now on I would let events take their own course and wait for 1965 to come around again. Never would there be so much lead in time to a first date as this. And so I bided my time and continued in my life as I now knew it, but this time with a daily sense of deja vu. That is not to say that every day I awoke I knew exactly what was going to happen that day, I didn't. But as the weeks slipped by I was confronted with situations and happenings that, as Sinatra sings, "seemed to be happening again."

As I ploughed through my life again my main preoccupation was Annette, and now that I knew she was Willie Rogers' girlfriend I began to get a bit uneasy about that relationship. I knew in the life I had come from I had nothing to worry about on that score, but this was all new and I did not know if the same conditions would prevail this time around. *After all they had a lot in common with their love of music and if Annette started to compose and write songs earlier than I had known her to, and Willie sang them, well, who knew what was likely to happen? What if, because of my interference, I had changed the dynamics in this life, and in effect I was helping to bring Annette and Willie Rogers together? Would my interference lead to Annette becoming the wife of Willie Rogers, and in that scenario what would become of me?*

It was not easy for me living through this time again, I had to act like a teenager though inside I was a man, with all the inclinations of a man who had the knowledge and experience that a lifetime of living brings. It would have been easy for me to exploit my situation and date girls, and I was tempted to at times, but I was deeply in love with Annette and believed that if I did anything inappropriate I would be unfaithful to her and this was something I was not prepared to do. In my first incarnation I did not frequent dance halls very much until I started going with Annette and I totally missed out on the sexual revolution taking place all around me. I used to joke that it all happened one night when I didn't go out. I only read about it all much later and was amazed that it all seemed to have passed me by. But now I could watch it as it passed me by.

Apart from winning a few pounds on bets I knew could not lose, and from time to time giving my da a winning tip, which this time around caused us to be closer than we had been the last time, I did not try in any way to influence or change events as I was fearful that anything I might do or say could have a butterfly effect and be responsible for causing other things to change, which in turn might have an effect on my future. I did not want my future to change, I wanted to get to that August Sunday 1965 intact, and finally relive my life with Annette.

I did not stray far from the life I had lived before, I continued to work for B&W, I continued to play football for St Saviour's. I went to Milltown to support Rovers most Sunday afternoons, and with my friends I went to Theatre Royal most Sunday nights. Some Sunday mornings when my mother thought I was at Mass I strolled down to the Ha'penny Bridge and stood looking at a supreme showman at work as he put on an exhibition of salesmanship that transfixed his audience and had them falling over themselves to be the first to buy his wares recently imported from the far away, and then still exotic, Orient.

Hector Grey was the forerunner of the pound and euro shops that proliferated later on and an entertainer supreme

– think of Del Boy with a Scottish accent – who set up shop amid a mountain of cardboard boxes and a large blue van every Sunday morning, on the open space between the Irish Woollen Mills and The Dublin Woollen Company beside the Ha'penny bridge. And as the saying goes, he could have sold ice to the Eskimos. I'm sure he would have made a fortune as a television personality if he had been born a bit later. He put on a show, for free, that would have filled many a theatre with paying customers.

As I went through the motions of reliving my life as a youth again, from time to time I thought of what the reaction would be if I had given in to the temptation that now and then came over me and I blurted out what I knew of events that were making the news headlines in the papers and the radio – but I didn't, I behaved as if it was all new to me.

Another line of thought that often entered my mind at this time, and it was something that worried me. *Was what were my family and friends doing and thinking now back in 2010? Where did they think I was? Was I listed as a missing person back there? Had they any idea what had happened to me? Did anyone see me rolling down the hill in the park that day? Did they see what happened when I reached the bottom? What had happened? Did I disappear in a puff of smoke, or was my elder self still lying in a heap at the bottom of the hill in the Phoenix Park?*

I had no idea.

To me the time between my lives was only a matter of a couple of months, but how long was it in reality? *Had I stepped outside the boundaries of time and space altogether and if I went back would I ever have existed at all? Would the life I remembered living back then be regarded as a figment of my imagination? Was it all my imagination? Which life was real, this one that I was only embarking on or the life I believed I had lived?*

These were the thoughts that were going through my mind as I endeavoured to live and behave as normally as I could, until the life I thought I had lived before could be put back on track; as I hoped it would be when I met Annette again in 1965.

Chapter eight

THE next few weeks were torture – knowing Annette was alive and only a bus journey from me tormented my mind and I was constantly thinking of ways I could see her again but still keep my promise that I would wait till 1965.

Then it came to me. I knew from my time with Annette, in our other life, that she was a fan of Adam Faith, the British rock singer and I had told her that I saw him when he came to Dublin in the early 60s. She said then that she would have loved to see him but she was living in Newbridge at the time and her parents would not let her go to Dublin on her own as she was too young. I remembered this when I saw the advertisement in the *Evening Herald* one night announcing that Adam Faith would be appearing at the Theatre Royal on the 7th of November. Back the first time around I had attended that show with my friend, Bunny Doyle, but I wondered this time around if Annette's liking for Adam Faith might be strong enough for her to overlook an intrusion by me back into her life before 1965? *Would it be possible for me to bring her to the show or would that be too much of an interference with time?*

I had not said anything to anyone, apart from Annette, about my time travelling exploits and as she already knew where I was coming from, so to speak, I pushed aside my reservations about the possible consequences for our future and booked two seats for the show.

True to form, shortly after doing so I met Bunny as we were both coming home from work one evening. He worked in a clothes shop on Talbot Street, and as he knew I was as big a fan of Adam Faith, as he was, he asked if I was going to see his show. I tried to suppress a smile as deja vu set in.

"I am," I said. "Are you?"

"If I can get a ticket, but I think they are all sold. Have you got one?" he replied.

"Yes, I have two."

"Who are you going with?" he asked.

"I'm not sure yet. I got one for a friend but I'm not sure if they'll be able to make it, they live in the country."

"If they can't go I'll buy it from you," he quickly replied.

So the scene was set, would history repeat itself or would time be altered and two lives be changed?

It was several weeks since I had made myself known to Annette and only a week from the show. In 1960 communication was not as easy as it had been in 2010, there were no texts, no Internet, no emails, no mobile phones, indeed not many phones of any kind and I knew Annette's home did not have a phone – nor did we. The only way to get in touch with her was by letter, or to take a bus trip to Newbridge.

So I threw caution to the wind and went to Newbridge. It was a Saturday and, like the last time, when I got there I headed straight to Kearns' Ice Cream Parlour, but Annette was not there. I walked up the main street until I came to the narrow lane that led into Pairc Mhuire and walked over to Annette's house. There was no sign of life about the house so I went to the front door, but before I knocked I looked through the window and got the shock of my life. Through the curtains I could see Annette and Willie Rogers on the sofa locked in an embrace, kissing. I was momentarily frozen on the spot, my wife kissing another man! And she seemed to be enjoying it. I was enraged and felt like barging in and dragging Rogers away from her, but just as I was about to bang on the window I realised that she was not my wife, not yet anyway, and tried to compose myself. They had not seen me so I moved away from the window and tried to calm down. I stood for about a minute to let my anger subside before approaching the door and giving three sharp knocks on the brass doorknocker. A few moments passed but the door remained firmly closed so I knocked again, this time louder and with more aggression. Eventually the door slowly opened and Rogers' head appeared in the opening. He looked surprised to see me and for a moment he did not open the door any further than about six or seven inches, just enough to see who was there. He looked confused as we both stared into each other's face, mine with an expression of unbridled anger.

"What do you want?" he asked, as he tried to assess the situation.

"Is Annette there?" I responded, with the anger I was trying to conceal forcing its way back into my demeanour.

"What do you want her for?" *I don't have to explain to you when I want to talk to my wife* I was thinking, but instead I bit my tongue and said, "Can I see her for a moment?"

Annette must have heard the conversation and came to the door, opening it wide as she stood beside Rogers.

"I didn't think you were coming back, what do you want?"

"Can I talk to you for a minute? Alone." The anger, at being forced to speak to my wife in this way, was welling up inside me.

Rogers looked at Annette and said, "You don't have to talk to him if you don't want to."

This was too much. I lunged forward and pulled him, by the collar of his shirt, from behind the door and he fell off balance onto the ground. I then stepped into the hall and as he sat on the ground in a state of bewilderment I stood beside a confused Annette and closed the door.

He just managed to regain some of his composure and picked himself up off the ground before starting to bang, with his fists on the closed door, while shouting, "What the fuck do you think you're doing? Let me in. If you hurt her I'll fucking kill you, you Dublin jackeen bastard."

As he was banging and shouting I said to Annette, "I'm not going to hurt you, I just want to talk to you. Will you get rid of him for a while so we can talk? Please?"

Annette looked distressed and said, "You said you would wait until 1965 to see what would happen, why are you back now? You might be ruining the future by what you're doing."

When she said this I looked at her, put my arms around her and said, "Then you believe me? You believe we shared a life together, that we were married and raised a family. You believe that somehow I travelled back through time from 2010 to be with you again, you believe that don't you?"

She released herself from my embrace and said, "I don't know what to believe, I'm confused. You walk into my life and tell me I was married to you in another life and say things about my family you should not know, things about me and the future. What you said the last time you were here about Mammy…she's pregnant like you said she would be and she wants to move back to Dublin and Daddy has been for an interview for a job and—"

"He'll get it," I interjected quickly. "Please can we talk?" All the while Rogers was banging on the door and shouting obscenities at me.

"Can you get rid of him?" I said looking to the door.

"OK, I'll try" she said, and once again I saw a glimmer of my wife, in her voice and action.

She opened the door and Rogers barged in with fists flying. He made a lunge at me, which I ducked away from as Annette shouted at him to stop, but he was not listening and made another lunge at me, which caught me on the shoulder and knocked me against the wall, shouting as he did so.

"You fucking Dublin jackeen, I'll kill you so I will."

"Stop it will you, Willie?" Annette shouted as she got between us. "He won't hurt me, he only wants to talk."

"What about, fucking highballs?" Willie retorted as his eyes bored into me. I moved away as Annette led Rogers into the front room and closed the door, leaving me standing in the hall. A few minutes later the door opened again and they both came out, Willie holding a guitar. He did not say anything as he eyed me up and down and I returned his stare with confidence.

"Will I see you later?" he then said to Annette, as he stood at the open door.

"I don't know" she replied, turning her gaze to me. I felt more confident about the situation now and as Rogers took a step away he turned and glared – a look of sheer anger and frustration on his face.

"My Mammy and Daddy will be back soon," Annette said as we went into the front room. They went shopping up the town with Liam and Marie and Claire."

"What are you going to tell them about me?" I asked her.

"What do you want me to tell them? That you're my husband and you've come to bring me home to do the cooking and iron your shirts?" she answered mischievously.

"Better not, not just yet," I laughed. "I haven't even asked Bill for your hand in marriage yet. What an ordeal you put me through with that the last time." I was beginning to feel very comfortable with Annette and I felt she was feeling the same way with me. It was starting to feel like our relationship used to, lots of talk and laughs with the words coming very easily.

"Tell me about it," she said and sat on the couch in front of the fireplace.

"About what?"

"About asking my Daddy for my hand." We were sitting on the couch in front of the fire, which was not lighting, but had a brightly coloured fireguard in place, and as she spoke she moved close to me. I put my arm around her shoulder and tears of happiness rolled down my face as I remembered how we used to sit like this on the couch in Tallaght.

"It was a Sunday night," I began. "Shortly after Christmas 1966. I had asked you to marry me at Christmas and you said yes, but you insisted that I ask your father before we formally announced our intentions. I was real nervous about asking him and had put it off for as long as I could, but you kept ribbing me about it and eventually I could put it off no longer. I did not normally see you on Sunday night, but for some reason you wanted me to ask that night. So I came out to Ballyfermot, you were living there at the time, and when I got there your mother and father had gone down the road to Young's, that's the pub they drank... will drink in, so I had to wait until they came back. Your two yet-to-be-born sisters, Caroline and Louise were in the house and we played and watched television with them until you decided it was time for them to go to bed. Eventually after ten o'clock your parents came home..." I paused and looked at Annette, she had her head on my shoulder and her eyes were wide open, with a look on her face as if she was living every word I was saying, so I continued.

"As soon as they came in, as if you had planned it, you got up off the couch we were sitting on and went into the kitchen with your mother, leaving me and your father in the front room. I think we both knew what was coming, but at least your father had had a few pints to steady his nerves while I was stone cold sober. Neither of us said anything for a while as your father poked the fire, just for something to do, while I sat contemplating just what I was going to say. I knew you and your mother were in the kitchen listening to anything that was said so I cleared my throat and as your father looked at me expectantly I said, "Annette's pregnant."

Suddenly Annette came out of her reverie and pulling her head off my shoulder looked at me and exclaimed, "What? What did you just say?!"

I looked at her and laughed, "Only joking!"

She visibly, immediately, relaxed and we both laughed as I held her tight.

"No, I didn't say that," I laughed. "I was very formal and respectful as I asked if we had his permission to get married."

"And what did he say?" Annette asked with excitement.

"He said no, so we eloped." I joked again.

"Oh stop it. Be serious, what did he say?"

"Ah yeah, that's all right," I said, mimicking her father. "I think he was glad to get rid of you."

Although Annette was only fourteen and I had the mind and intellect of a mature man I could feel the old chemistry taking over and we were gelling like I remembered we used to, the intellectual age gap was being filled. We were becoming soulmates again.

As these thoughts were going through my mind I turned to Annette who, once again, had placed her head on my shoulder as if it was the most natural thing in the world for her to do and dispensing with the levity I asked, "Annette, do you believe me now? Do you believe what I'm telling you, that we once shared a life in another time, that you were, are my wife?"

She remained with her head on my shoulder and without moving answered. "I can't take it all in, what you are saying about travelling through time is not possible, yet I don't understand how you can know all the things you do know about me and my family. It's not possible for anyone to come from 2010 to 1960."

Then lifting her head from my shoulder and looking straight into my eyes she pleaded, "Is it?" And I knew she wanted it to be.

"I did," I said simply.

"I just don't know. You could be making it all up."

"Why would I do that, and how would I know all the things I do know about you and your family unless I got that knowledge by living with you in another life?" I said, beginning to feel exasperated at her for having such doubts after all I'd told her. "I told you you'd have more sisters before you knew your mother was pregnant. I told you you'd return to Dublin when your father got a job there and you've just told me that he has been for a job interview… in International Saws on the quays, is that right? That's where he will work in Dublin, and you didn't tell me the name of the company he went for the interview to, did you? How could I know all these things unless I've…we've lived through them. I swear Annette I'm telling you the truth."

She disengaged herself from me and I could see tears in her eyes.

"What's the matter, why are you crying?" I asked.

"If this is all true then what's the point of me? What's the point of my life if what you are saying is true? I have no choice in how I live it from here on. It's all mapped out for me, no matter what I want to do I can't change what you know is in store for me, isn't that so? If what you're saying is true I have no say in the matter, so from here on I might as well just tag along with you and let things happen as if I was a puppet or a rag doll." She appeared dejected.

I was taken aback and surprised by her words, which were so much deeper and more intellectually penetrating than any fourteen-year-old should have been able to provide. I should not have been surprised though, they were exactly the words the Annette I came back to be with would have spoken. I held her hand and tried to think what to say to her that would make any sense of the situation we were in.

"I don't pretend to understand this either" I began. "I don't know how or why it happened or if I have caused things to change by making myself known to you sooner than we are destined to meet. I don't know what will happen to us between now and August 1965, I did not know you in 1960 the last time. What happens to us between now and then I have no idea."

"That's not what I'm worried about, I have some control over that. It's what you're saying is going to happen after 1965 that worries me" she replied.

We sat in silence for a while and then Annette turned to me and asked, "Why did you come back now? I thought you were going to wait till 1965?"

With all that had happened I'd forgotten about that.

"Oh that, with my duet with Willie Rogers I forgot all about what I'm here for." I told her.

"What do you mean, your duet with Willie?" she asked

"Forget it," I said. "It's just a figure of speech. You like Adam Faith don't you? How would you like to see him live in concert?"

"How do you know… Oh I suppose I told you that too did I?"

"Yes," I laughed. "You missed him the last time he was here in 1960, He's on the Theatre Royal next week and I have two tickets for the show, it's a great show, or at least it was the last time I saw it, would you like to come to it?"

"With you?"

"Yes, who else? I'm certainly not giving Rogers the tickets, it's not his kind of music"

"Did I go with you the last time?"

"No."

"Then I don't think I should go this time."

Even as a fourteen-year-old she had more sense and intelligence than I had on my second life, as soon as she said it I knew she was right.

"You'll never change," I told her. "You'll always be more insightful than I'll ever be. You're right, we shouldn't try to change what's already happened"

"Who did you go with the last time?" she asked curiously.

"A friend of mine, Bunny Doyle," I told her.

"Bunny? That's a funny name, is it a boy or a girl?"

I laughed as I remembered Annette asking the exact same thing the first time I mentioned my friend's name to her in our last life.

"It's a boy, his real name is Martin," I said. And then knowing what she was going to say next, I mimicked her as she said, *"Then why don't you call him Martin?"*

I laughed as I looked at the bemused look on her face and said "I know you so well, those are the exact words you spoke the last time I told you Bunny was a boy. Bunny is just a nickname."

Then there was a noise at the door and for a moment I thought Rogers was back and I prepared to defend myself if he got aggressive again, but then I heard a woman's voice.

"Are you in Annette, is Willie still here?" I recognised Mary's voice, softer than I remembered it though, as she had not started smoking yet. She only started smoking after Bill's death in 1970 so the huskiness that developed in later years was not there yet.

"Its Mammy and Daddy back from the shops" Annette said and I took my arm from around her shoulder and stood up. Annette remained sitting on the couch as I looked at her pleadingly for guidance as to what to do or say. Although I was intellectually years older than Annette I immediately reverted to looking to her to lead the way in what we should do next – exactly as I always did in our other life. I depended on her so much, even now.

"I'm in the front room Mammy," Annette called out as Mary opened the door. Mary was then almost forty years old, a good-looking woman with blond hair, she was wearing a blue Macintosh type coat over a white cardigan and dark blue skirt, and was showing the early signs of her pregnancy. Bill was taking the shopping out of the pram and was being helped by Marie and Liam while Claire was giving me the once over. When Mary saw me she hesitated coming any further and stood holding the door knob as her gaze shifted from me to Annette and then back to me. I looked to Annette with a pleading look that said, *"what do we do now?"*

Then as the silence was threatening to become tense Annette said, "Mammy this is Andy Halpin, he's from Dublin."

Mary relaxed a bit and called to Bill saying, "Bill, Annette has a friend with her...he's from Dublin."

Whereupon Bill put down the things he had in his hand and came into the room, followed closely by Marie and

Liam. Bill was exactly as I remembered him, a thin man with well oiled black hair, wearing a light brown coloured sports coat, a white open necked shirt with the shirt collar worn over his jacket collar and grey trousers and brown leather sandals on his feet, he was then in his early forties.

I stood and proffered my hand in greeting, which was taken first by Bill and then by Mary as she asked, "Where abouts in Dublin do you come from?"

"Wellington Street" I replied, "Lower Wellington Street."

"Where's that" Mary asked.

"It's near Dorset Street isn't it?" Bill said.

"That's right," I confirmed, "between Mountjoy Street and Dorset Street."

There was then an uneasy silence as we all stood waiting for someone to speak, and then Liam who was nine years old chipped in and broke the tension, "I'm going to play the guitar when I'm big."

I smiled and looked at Annette and said, "Do you know what Liam, you're going to play the guitar, the mandolin, the fiddle and lots of other instruments when you're big, so you are."

Realising that I had said his name and seeing Mary and Bill exchange looks I quickly added, "Annette was just telling me she had a little brother called Liam so I assume you're him, am I right?"

Liam then said in a way that suggested he was offended, "I'm not little, so I'm not."

As we smiled at his remark and Bill tossed his hair with his hand Mary said, "Oh don't be telling him that or he'll have us pestered wanting us to buy him all those instruments."

I looked over at Annette and said, "he will."

"Did you make your friend a cup of tea?" Bill asked Annette as she stood in silence. This was developing into an almost exact replica of the first time I met Mary and Bill in the 1965 timeframe, when myself and Annette were come upon by them as we were courting on the porch in Ballyfermot, back then Bill had invited me in for a cup of tea to what I thought was a reluctance on Annette's part. Here he was again suggesting I have a cup of tea and again Annette seemed reluctant to be hospitable.

"It's alright," I said "I have to catch the bus back to Dublin."

"What time is the bus at?" Bill asked.

"Five."

He looked at his watch and said, "Sure it's only gone four, you have plenty of time for a quick cup of tea, I'll put on the kettle."

I looked over at Annette who was totally impassive and not about to offer me encouragement to stay, then I smiled and said, "OK so, sure I have all the time in the world."

Mary and Bill then went into the kitchen bringing Marie, Claire and Liam with them and Annette and I sat back on the couch.

"What are you going to tell them about me?" I asked her when we were alone.

"I don't know, you're the one who knows the future," she replied in her best sarcastic voice.

"Ha ha, very funny. I told you I only know what's going to happen after August 1965, not now, this is all new to me too."

"Well you better think of something, because they'll want to know how I know someone from Dublin."

Before I could reply Mary came in with two cups of tea and some biscuits on a tray and laid them on a small coffee table in front of us.

"Did you come down to Newbridge on your own?" Mary asked me as she stood over us after putting the tray on the table.

"Eh no," I started to say trying hard to think of something that would sound convincing. "I came down with a friend who had a few songs for Willie Rogers."

Mary, looking at me with a quizzical look on her face, as I tried to think of what to say next asked suspiciously, "How did you know Willie Rogers?"

I sat with my heart racing trying to think how I knew Willie Rogers and then Annette interjected and said, "I told him about Willie when we met in Bray in the summer, when I went on that school trip."

"That's right," I said thankful that Annette had done what she had so often done in the past (or was that the future?) got me out of a tight spot. "That's right I met Annette in Bray in the summer and she was telling me about her friend Willie, that he was a good singer but he needed some new songs."

I lied and looked for a further response from Annette who remained impassive, that was as far as she was prepared to go.

"Songs for Willie Rogers?" Mary said with an air of disdain. "Sure he hasn't a note in his head."

"Ah give him time and he'll be OK," I responded.

"And where is he now?," she asked looking at Annette.

"Who?" Annette replied, not having been paying attention to the conversation.

"Willie. I thought you were going to the pictures with him?" Mary asked. Now it was my turn to rescue Annette.

"He's gone back to his house with my friend Jimmy McCarthy, to try out the songs" I interjected to save Annette having to explain what had happened earlier. "I'm meeting him there and then me and Jimmy are going back to Dublin" I lied.

"Are you?" she said, still rather suspicious. "And will you be coming back to Newbridge again?"

I looked over at Annette and smiled. "Who knows what will happen in the future? I might come back to Newbridge, or I might wait and go to Bray again."

Mary gave me an uncomprehending look and said, "Well have your cup of tea anyway," and as she was leaving the room said to Annette, "Don't keep him late for his bus."

When we were alone I said to Annette, "Do you know what, that was like history repeating itself, before it happened that is. What has just happened was almost exactly what happened the first time I met your parents in the other life, we were having a court on your doorstep in Ballyfermot when your parents came back from the pub and your father invited me in for a cup of tea, which you appeared not to be keen on, just like now, and your mother said exactly the same thing about you not keeping me late for my bus."

Annette got embarrassed about what I had just said about us courting and got up off the couch and said, "What was that about Willie getting songs from someone? Is he going to be famous some day?"

"Oh that. I just made it up. I had to say something and you told me he was into music so that was the first thing that came into my head." I lied.

She looked at me with one of her disbelieving looks and I was waiting for her to ask, *"Do you think I'm a complete fool?"* But she just said, "Well anyway I think you should go now. I won't be going to see Adam Faith with you, I don't think it would be right to do so. Do what you did the last time and go with your friend Martin."

I put the cup onto the table stood up and said, "I suppose you're right, no point in trying to change things too much. I'll carry on doing what I did before until..."

"Yeah, I think that's the best thing to do" Annette stopped me before I could finish the sentence.

I stood looking at her, fighting the urge to take her in my arms and kiss her. Sensing my heightened emotions she moved away from me and opened the door, standing beside it holding it open. I walked past her and as I did I held both her hands and kissed her gently on the lips.

"See you soon...Dix," I said, using a pet name I used to call her.

I stood and looked, one last time, into her eyes and said, "Tell your parents thanks for the tea." And I walked across the small grass patch in front of the house.

Before walking into the lane that led to the main street though, I turned and looked back.

Annette was still standing at the door looking after me.

Chapter nine

SOON it was Christmas 1960 and my mind was tortured by indecision again. *Should I make contact with Annette or wait as I had said I would for destiny to decide our fate?* I wanted to see her so much, but I did not want to be seen to be putting pressure on her and risk what I knew was to be our future. I was not easy to live with over this period. I was moody and irritable and kept my distance from my friends because I had outgrown their interests. I had long ago passed through that phase and had worn and discarded the t-shirt of my youth.

I did not drink alcohol in my last life until I was eighteen or nineteen but now trying to get through this period I was sorely tempted to have a drink. Because of my physical age, however, that would have been almost impossible as very few, if any, pubs would have served me. The age of rampant underage drinking had not arrived yet. Off-licences were few and far between and they, likewise, were unlikely to serve someone as young as I now was. The advent of the proliferation of Tesco, Aldi, Lidl and Dunnes Stores was only a dot on the horizon. It was hard at times to maintain my persona as a fifteen-year-old with the turmoil that was going on in my mind over Annette and I now also had to worry about her relationship with Willie Rogers. Though I tried to convince myself that that was only a passing phase as I pretty well knew how his life was going to pan out and it did not include Annette. Still things might not be quite the same this time around. She had asked me if Willie was going to be famous and if I did not convince her that her future was with me before Willie began his ascent to stardom it might be too late, as she might be carried along with him on his rise to fame and fortune.

All these things were going through my mind in the run up to that Christmas back in 1960.

I passed a lot of the time walking around the city looking at the shop windows all decked out in seasonal fare and was amused by the contrast in what was on display compared to the technological gadgetry like computers, Xboxes, PlayStations, 50-inch television sets and an array of mobile phones, which were all the rage in the time I had come from.

Sometimes as I stood looking at a window display I was pretending to be interested in my mind would start wandering and I'd find myself glancing at the people all around me; and the thought often entered my head; *Are any of them like me? Are any of them caught in a time warp, somehow having been transported from another time and place and not knowing why or how they got here?*

I sometimes wondered what would have happened if I had engaged some of those window shoppers in conversation and during the course of our discussion asked, "Does the name Osama Bin Laden mean anything to you? How about 9-11? Or President Barak Obama of the United States, have you ever heard of him? Have you ever taken a trip on the Luas or Dart? What about iPhones, laptops or iPads, are you missing them in this Internet-free world?"

Would I get uncomprehending looks as people hurried to walk away from me or would I be embraced and befriended by a fellow confused and frightened time traveller?

I surely could not be the only one experiencing a trip through time, could I? This must have happened to, or be happening to others, who like me now, lacked the courage to make themselves known – or were all those people who claimed to be Napoleon, Cleopatra, The Tsar of Russia and such like, for real?

Another thing that puzzled me then was, where was the other Andrew? The one I displaced in this age. The one who was too sick to go to work the day I arrived. *Where was he? Had he replaced me in 2010? And if he had how would he cope with being transported into an age of such technological advances?* He would have no knowledge of the life others would have remembered him living, or of all that happened in the world between 1960 and 2010.

Would he have the intellect of a fifteen-year-old boy in the body of a sixty-five-year old man and would he be looking for a long-demolished tenement building in Wellington Street, calling out for his mother and father?

And when he was confronted by his family would he be unable to recognise them? Would they think he has lost control of his mind, brought on by the grief of losing his wife, a wife he never knew. How would a fifteen-year-old boy cope with all that?

All these things were going through my mind as I did my best to come to terms with the situation I found myself in, and tried to act as normal as it is possible for an elderly man locked into an adolescent body.

I bought a Christmas card just before Christmas with the intentions of sending it to Annette in Newbridge, but after writing the Christmas greetings I wished to convey to her on the card and putting it in an envelope I decided not to send it to her Newbridge address, but instead put our Tallaght address on the envelope and dropped it into a letterbox.

How long, I wondered, *would it take the P&T to deliver this Christmas card?!*

I did all the things I must have done in the other timeframe over that Christmas period. I went with my friends to see Jack Cruise in *Christmas Cruise* in the Theatre Royal, had *Melancholy Babies* in the Palm Grove Cafe on O'Connell Street and went to the Savoy to see the new Norman Wisdom film, *The Bulldog Breed*. And through it all I wondered, *was it really this dull and boring the last time?*

It had its good points though, it was great getting the chance to spend another Christmas with my parents and brother and to see all my aunts and uncles again. I used to annoy Annette in the other timeframe, when I'd say that no one could make a Christmas pudding like my mother, and tasting it again after so long only confirmed my belief – it was even better than I remembered. She made it the old-fashioned way, with lots of Guinness and whiskey, mixed peel and spices, and boiled it all night on the old gas cooker wrapped in a muslin cloth in a big aluminium pot. The aroma that pervaded the entire house when it was cooking was heavenly. Served with hot *Bird's Custard* it was delicious. Her ham was also cooked to perfection, and Annette, while she may have disagreed with me about the pudding, got to love her ham and looked forward to going to the flat on Bank Holiday weekends when my mother always cooked it.

I can't remember what, or if, I bought my parents Christmas presents the last time, but this time I bought them the best presents I could afford. A royal blue silk blouse and a white cardigan for my mother from *The Silk Mills* in Dorset Street and a box of fifty *Woodbines* and a silver *Zippo* lighter for my father.

I bought my brother Joe a big lead figure circus set because

I remembered that at some time in another existence I had broken a set belonging to him when we had a row about something or other.

The money for all these presents, I got from having Liam Stephens place a bet for me on a horse called *Knuckle Kracker* in the *Hennessy Gold Cup*, which was being run at Newbury for the first time shortly before Christmas. It was a bet I knew I could not lose. I did not do that very often, but it was handy now and then when I was short of cash and I remembered the result of some sporting event, usually football, but also when some of the big race meetings came around and I remembered the names of the horses. For his trouble Liam made a few pounds as well.

I remember on one occasion after a horse – an outsider at 25/1 – that I had Liam place a bet on for me, won, as he gave me my winnings he asked in jest, "Have you been here before?"

"Yeah," I replied. "Did I not tell you?"

But throughout the whole time my mind was preoccupied with Annette and I had to fight, very hard, the urge to jump on a bus and go to Newbridge. I did not know how I was going to contain that urge for the next four and a half years. I was constantly thinking and wondering how the relationship with Willie Rogers was developing and my mind could not rid itself of the sight of them kissing in the front room in Pairc Mhuire. I was tormented by it, but I took some consolation from Annette's attitude when I was leaving her in October. While not saying that she believed me, she did seem to indicate that she was open to believing what I was telling her. This was solace to me. Comfort in believing that she would, at some point, accept that we had shared a life together, especially when her father got the job I told he would get in International Saws and the family moved back to Dublin.

I had told her of her mother's pregnancy before it happened, and also that the baby would be a girl and that she would be called Caroline. This prophecy would soon be fulfilled, and I hoped it would also help to bolster my credentials with Annette.

I did not know exactly when the Kennedys moved to Dublin, but I knew it was sometime in 1961 or early '62, and I knew that when they did Annette and I would be working very close to each other for maybe a year and a half. She would be working in O'Dea's, the mattress makers on the corner of Wolf Tone Street and Mary Street and I would be working about a hundred yards further up Mary Street in Burroughs & Watts. I had not told her that in the conversations we had, but thinking about it now, I was pretty sure I must have seen her at sometime during that period of the '65 timeframe, before we met in Bray.

I remembered particularly one day at lunchtime when I was walking back to work and I noticed an attractive young girl walking on the other side of Capel Street. I was attracted to her appearance. She seemed to stand out from the crowd and we both looked at each other as we passed, our eyes seeming to lock for a second or two before we both got embarrassed and our eye embrace disengaged. I distinctly remembered it was as if we knew each other. *Was that Annette?* I now wondered. I don't know.

Another place we could have met without knowing it, before meeting in Bray, was a little dairy shop in Denmark Street, which was run by an elderly lady, Mrs Murphy, I think was her name. She wore her hair in a bun and a blue wraparound shop apron. It was a shop all on its own on a patch of waste ground where people from the numerous small clothing factories and workshops around the area used go each morning to get milk, tea, cakes, broken biscuits and loose cigarettes for the morning breaks. We had discovered, from talking about ourselves in the last life, that both of us used to, on occasion, go to this shop – Annette to get the provisions for O'Dea's and me for B&W. Incidentally Annette told me a great story about how she used to make a few pennies profit on those shopping trips. Instead of buying loose cigarettes she'd buy a packet of ten, which was a few pence cheaper than buying the cigarettes loose, divvy them out to those who had paid her to buy maybe one or two cigarettes and keep the difference in the price. With all her Christian values she never saw anything wrong in doing that.

The shop was always packed with young boys and girls eyeing each other up and I'm sure we must have been in there at the same time on one or two mornings, though neither of us remembered seeing each other when we spoke about it in the last life. Quite possibly we may have stood beside each other, giving each other discrete glances, too shy to make eye contact.

Another thing Annette told me in the '65 timeframe, when our relationship had developed, (and when I thought about it now gave me great confidence and a belief that we were always meant to be together) was that the first morning she went to work in O'Dea's, after walking from the bus stop on Aston's Quay and passing up to one hundred shops, when she got to the corner of Wolf Tone Street and Abbey Street she noticed a small shoemakers shop with the name *Halpin* over the door and she paused at it and thought it was a very strange name. She told me that she pronounced the name to herself as Hal-pin and was struck by how the name sounded. She told me she had never heard the name before, but the fact that she had noticed it, out of all the shops she had passed after getting off the bus, started me thinking now that maybe she had in fact heard it before – and somewhere deep in her subconscious the name subliminally awakened something of a "future memory." *Were our lives a series of repetitions, a continuous stream of deja vus? I wondered. Were we destined to forever repeat our lives over and over again in different timeframes or dimensions?*

I could live with that if all my lives were with Annette and if this was the hand that destiny has dealt me, a perpetual time traveller with Annette as my companion, then I was truly fortunate.

I somehow managed to keep my word to Annette. I did not go back to Newbridge again, but I did manage to see her. I did not know exactly when the Kennedy's moved to Dublin apart from the fact that it was in 1961/62, but I knew that when they did Annette was fifteen years of age and her mother got her a job she did not want in O'Dea's. The Annette of the '65 era told me she would have loved to train as a dress designer, a job she knew she would have excelled at, but family finances dictated otherwise and she ended up as an apprentice upholsterer in the factory her mother worked in before she was married.

I knew Annette would not be fifteen until August 1961, so it had to be after that when she began working in O'Dea's. The first time I saw her, after she came to Dublin was a total surprise and a shock to me. I was not expecting it at all when it happened. It was a warm sunny day in early September, a Friday as I remember it. I was returning to B&W at about a 1.45pm, having finished my service calls early. My last call had been to the Officers Mess in Collins Barracks and, it being a fine sunny day, I decided to walk back along the quays and up Capel Street, saving the bus fare I was allowed for the call. As I approached Slattery's pub on the corner of Capel Street and Mary's Lane, and I was about to cross the road, I noticed a few girls eating ice cream cones and walking a little ahead of me on the opposite side of the street. I thought one of them looked familiar and as I drew parallel with them and was about to cross the street I recognised the unmistakable face of Annette. It had been almost a year since I last saw her and I was awe struck at how grown up she now looked compared to the young girl in a school uniform she had been the last time I met her.

She was wearing black patent shoes with a higher heel than the school shoes she had been wearing in Newbridge, which gave a more mature look to her legs, which were exposed to above her knees in a tight black mini skirt. She also had a white blouse opened at the neck with long sleeves, which she had pulled up around her tanned arms. Her hair was in a bouffant style, high on her head, which emphasised her face, on which I could see she had begun to wear makeup. She looked much older than the fifteen-year-old I knew her to be.

Although I knew I was going to see Annette again I was not prepared for it happening like this. I had thought it would be, and wanted it to be, at a time and place of my choosing, when I could control and dictate events. I was not ready for this, especially seeing how mature she looked. I was reduced to the shy awkward youth I used to be in my last incarnation. She did not see me, I was sure of that so I quickly changed direction and turned down Little Mary Street instead of crossing the road. I walked quickly away from Annette and her friends until I was about a hundred yards down the street. I then stopped and turned and looked back up the street towards the corner of Capel Street – the girls were not there anymore.

I was surprised at how shaken I had been at seeing

Annette again, and at how grown up she looked. *But why was I so surprised? It had been almost a year since I last saw her. What was I expecting?* She was not a school girl any longer, she was developing into the beautiful young girl I met and fell for in Bray in 1965.

I walked slowly back towards Capel Street, my mind racing with excitement at how great Annette looked now, but also confused about what I should do next. She looked so mature and grown up since the last time I saw her and I still looked like an awkward sixteen-year-old, which I had been trying to be so as to blend into my situation. *But was I succeeding too well?*

As I walked passed O'Dea's I quickly crossed the road without a backward glance, continued up Mary Street and into the safety of B&W. I gave in my service reports and stored my case and equipment away for the weekend, had a few words with Liam and Tom who were also finishing up early as it was a Friday, before we all left by the back gate in Chapel Lane, which led out onto Parnell Street.

We said our goodbyes at the top of the lane and went our separate ways. I had, by then, moved to the new flats in Dominick Street, so I only had a short distance to walk, which I did with my head, totally confused about what I should do now that Annette was in Dublin. I knew I would meet her again now that we were working so close to each other, but I did not want it to be by chance like we almost met today. I wanted to orchestrate the next meeting so that I would be able to control the situation and not be at a disadvantage, as I would have been earlier, had Annette seen me. Using the vernacular of a future time, I decided it would be a no-brainer not to use the advantage I had and actually prevent things happening by chance again. I should use that advantage to set up a meeting with Annette that would make it seem like pure chance. Just how I would do that I had no idea. I knew the promise I had made to her, to let things take their own course and not contact her again until we met in 1965, was not now going to happen. Now that I had seen her, and how great she looked, I wanted to be with her, at once. I was still concerned at how our coming together at this time would affect our future life together, but not enough to stop me conspiring to somehow meet her again. I wanted to be able to hold her and kiss her again and I was prepared to believe that our meeting now would have no effect on our future as I remembered it. I could think of nothing else that weekend only Annette, and at one point I even walked to the 78 bus stop on Aston's Quay in the hope I would see her if she came into town. I was behaving like the adolescent my appearance portrayed me to be, not the mature man that inhabited my body.

After a very confused and restless weekend I set out for work on Monday morning determined that I would be with Annette before the week was out – though I still had not worked out how this would come about. I could just be brave and bold and wait outside O'Dea's some evening or I could "accidently" bump into her some lunch hour when I knew she often went for a walk around Capel Street. My inclination was not to antagonise Annette by a show of bravado, but to try and meet her by "chance." Also on my mind was her relationship with Willie Rogers and how that was going since she came to live in Dublin.

Monday turned to Tuesday and Tuesday to Wednesday and soon it was the weekend again but I still had not figured out a way of "accidentally" meeting Annette. I went to the little dairy in Denmark Street a few mornings during the week, in the hope that Annette would be there, but no luck. I knew that all I had to do was to be outside O'Dea's some evening at half five and I was sure to meet her, but I wanted to make our meeting, when it did happen, seem like chance as I felt that in this way Annette would not be annoyed with me and think I was breaking my word to her by trying to manipulate things to my advantage. I knew I could not go on like this much longer, knowing how close she was and how much I wanted to be with her again was torture. I had to arrange a "chance" meeting soon or, I felt, I'd go mad.

Then fate took over and we really did meet by chance. After two weeks of indecision and procrastination on my part, one Monday morning as I was crossing the Ha'penny Bridge on my way to St Stephens Green to service billiard tables in a gentlemen's clubs, I saw her. She was walking briskly towards me on the bridge, her hair high on her head covered in a red scarf and wearing a loose-fitting beige coloured coat that I remembered she had in our last time together. I could not believe my eyes, I had been racking my brains trying to think of a way to bring about a situation like this and here she was, literally walking into my arms.

As she approached me I stopped walking and could not prevent a big smile developing on my face. I placed my case on the ground and held out my arms to her. "Annette," I said. "It's great to see you again, how are you?"

She stopped walking, short of my outstretched arms and seemed surprised to see me. For a moment I was not sure she recognised me and I let my arms fall by my side as it was obvious she was not going to come any closer.

Again I said, " It's great to see you again Annette, how have you been?"

Then when she showed no response to my greeting I said, "You do know me don't you?"

A slight smile came over her face and she replied, "Yes, of course I know you. You're my husband aren't you?"

"Will be," I replied and smiled back at her, then, "Where are you going?"

"I'm late for work," she said.

"Some things never change."

"What do you mean by that?" she sounded slightly miffed.

"Nothing. It's all ahead of us."

"Mammy had a baby, it was a girl and she called her... Caroline."

"And Daddy got a job in International Saws?" I asked, a glint in my eye.

"Yes," she replied rather timidly. "And we're living with my aunt Hanna at the moment, until we get our own house. That's why I'm late for work, there's too many in the house and I couldn't get into the bathroom this morning to get ready."

"All exactly as I told you it would be then," I said. "And I kept my word too, I did not go to Newbridge again... although I dearly wanted to."

"Yes, I know you did," she replied.

"So now that we've met by chance..."

"Did you know that we'd meet like this? Did you set this up?" Her question stopped me before I could finish.

"No, of course not. I told you before, I don't know what happens between us until 1965. I did not know you at this time in the last timeframe, this meeting is as much a surprise to me as it is to you. I had no idea I would see you this morning, but now that we have, well...would you like to...come out with me tonight?"

She stood looking at me and I knew she was thinking hard and considering whether to accept the invitation or not. Then she said, "I don't think we should."

"Why?" I asked "are you still seeing Willie Rogers?"

"No, that's all over. Willie was more interested in his music than he was in me. He has not been in touch since we moved to Dublin."

Well, I thought. *That's a relief. It's his loss though, you could have supplied him with some great songs.*

"Then why not come out with me, just once, that's all and then I promise I won't see you again until…" I trailed off.

"I don't know, it would not be right to do so, it might… "Well we don't know what might happen do we?" I held her hands and said, "Annette I know what happens to us after 1965 and it's mostly good. Nothing can change that, please come out with me now and let's take things from here. 1965 doesn't matter anymore now anyway. It can't be as it was, we…I have changed all that. I don't want to waste anymore time, I want to be with you now."

"I'm dead late for work," she replied, ignoring what I had said. "I really have to go."

As she stepped away from me and walked down the slope of the bridge I called after her, "I'll meet you at the 78 bus stop at eight o'clock tomorrow night. Don't be late!"

Chapter ten

SHE was, exactly as she had been on our first date in 1965. I stood waiting on Aston's Quay for almost thirty minutes before Annette stepped off a 78 bus with her auburn hair now loose on her head, pushed back behind her ears. She was wearing a light dusty blue jacket and knee-length skirt over a flower pattern blue blouse and black medium heeled shoes while carrying a black bag with a short strap and an umbrella. She looked great, and all I could do was reach out, take her hand and shake my head, smiling.

"What are you smiling about?" she wanted to know.

"You, you're so consistent. You never changed," I replied.

"I don't know what you mean."

"Come on, where would you like to go?"

I led her away from the bus stop forgetting for a moment that this was 1961 and we were two teenagers, back then teenagers did not frequent bars in anything like the way they did in 2010. And some bars still did not admit or serve women! So our choice of venue for our date was somewhat limited.

"I don't know, what had you in mind?" she asked and held my hand as we walked towards O'Connell Bridge.

"I've had nothing but you on my mind since I last saw you," Annette got a bit embarrassed by my intensity so I just laughed and added, "Would you like to see Elvis? *Flaming*

Star is on the Capitol. It's the last of his good films. After this, apart from *Blue Hawaii*, it's all downhill."

"What do you mean?" she asked.

"You'll see," I said. "Col Parker only wants the money."

"You say the strangest things," she said. "I don't know what you mean at times."

"The future is a strange place," I smiled.

"Will we get in to the Capitol now? It's late and the film will have started?" she asked as we made our way up O'Connell Street.

"Come on we'll try." I quickened the pace.

Turning off O'Connell Street at the Metropole we could see that there was a small queue at the steps of the Capitol, but it was moving so we joined it and very soon we were at the box office.

"Two one and nines please," I said as I pushed a 10 shilling note under the glass panel and the cashier pressed her button before the tickets shot up from under the brass coloured panel in front of me. The cashier then gave me six shillings and six pence change.

We quickly made our way into the parterre where we were met by an usher with a torch who guided us to two empty seats in the middle of a row about halfway from the screen. The credits were just beginning to appear on the screen for the main feature and I told Annette to take her seat as I went over to the girl selling ice cream and sweets from the wooden tray slung around her neck. I bought two tubs and a bag of Double Centres, all for one and nine pence. I made my way back to Annette and sat beside her before giving her the sweets and a tub. I had seen the film before so I spent most of the time looking at Annette and her reaction to it. Annette was, I remembered, the type of filmgoer who got caught up in the story of the film and lived every scene, so when Elvis died at the end I was expecting waterworks.

The Capitol had been the setting for our first date in 1965 too, then it was Frank Sinatra in *Von Ryan's Express* who provided the entertainment. Now on our first date in this timeframe we were in the Capitol again, but watching Elvis.

Just like 1965 I did not attempt to become over familiar with Annette but just basked in the joy of being in her company again and held her hand. I could see she was engrossed in and enjoying the film and that was pleasure enough for me. It was after10.30pm when the film ended so we had not got much time for talking before the last bus at 11.30pm.

After confirming that she had enjoyed the film I suggested we go for a cup of coffee before catching her bus so we went to The Rainbow Cafe near O'Connell Bridge, which was also close to the bus stop, so we could stay until the last minute. After ordering coffee and cakes I reached over and took Annette's hand.

"What now, what do we do now?"

"I've really enjoyed tonight and I like your company, but I don't know…things like you've told me just don't happen. People can't travel through time… and even if it's true and somehow you did manage to… we can't meet for the first time in 1965 now, so what happens from then can't be as you remember it. Things will have to be different between us, can't you see that?"

I had to concede that she was right.

"That may be true, and our future may not now be exactly as I remember it, but that's all the better. We'll both be experiencing it together for the first time. Though I'm sure it will follow closely how it was, we'll marry and have our children who are alive and well in 2010, and we'll lead a very happy life."

"I don't know. By what you've done you have changed all that, nothing can now be as you say it was. When 1965 comes around we'll have already met, and if we continue to see each other our relationship will be almost five years old. It will not be, cannot be, in any way as you say it was. We may be fed up with each other by then and I'll have the right to marry or not marry anyone I wish. If my future ever was with you, by your action you have changed that and given me my life back, to lead as I so desire. Not as you have told me it will be."

This was not what I was expecting tonight. The Annette I remembered and loved was disintegrating before my very eyes. Had I destroyed everything I was hoping for by my hasty and ill-considered actions?

"What are you saying, that you will not marry me? That you will not give birth to our children? Children that are already alive in another time. Annette I loved you so much that I came back to be with you and live our life all over again, that's all I ever wanted to do, to love you and be with you."

As I tried to think of something else to say to retrieve the situation she said, "How did you come back? I mean what happened, you never told me what happened. Just that something caused you to travel back through time, but what was it, what caused it?" Annette asked as the waitress placed the coffee and cakes on the table.

I was worried by the change I now perceived in her and knew I had to be honest or I was in danger of it all ending right then. But how honest could I be with her? I was not going to tell her she had passed away, of that I was certain. But I knew I had to tell her something and it had to be convincing so I tried to gather my thoughts and said, "It would be unfair of me to tell you everything about our life together from our first meeting in 1965, so I am not going to do so. What I will tell you is that it was a good life, we were, for the most part, very happy. Sure we had our moments and there were times when things were not all sunshine and roses. Like everyone else we hurt each other from time to time, and I have to put my hand up and admit that I hurt you more than you ever hurt me, but I want you to know that I always loved you and I have never stopped loving you. I never set out to, or intentionally, hurt you. I was very stupid and careless from time to time and caused you hurt and pain for which I am so sorry, but overall our life was very happy. We raised a good family and they were a credit to you – to the way you brought them up by deed and example.

I continued, "We were never rich, but we did not want for the essentials and always had more than enough to get by. In 2009 something, which at this time I don't want to talk about, happened. Something which may or may not happen in this timeframe, but now that I'm aware of it, I will, when that time comes, be in a position to do something about it should the same set of circumstances prevail. That is why I am not going to speak of it now. This event had a profound effect on me and I believe it caused me to enter a state of mind that contributed to my travelling back through time. One minute I was a sixty-five-year-old man and then, all of a sudden, I found myself back in 1960 – a fifteen-year-old youth. That's really as much as I can tell you now, but I really want you to believe me Annette, because it's all true. I swear to you it is and I would never deceive you."

She remained silent for a few moments, then, "I don't know what to believe, there's something about you that tells me you are telling the truth, but if you are I keep asking myself where does that leave me? It means that my life is already lived and if it goes on as you remember it I have no choice in how I live it. I can't do anything to change the future you know is ahead of me if I remain with you. I'll have no free will or discretion in how I live my life. My life will only be an excuse for you to relive yours.

She added, "You seem to have had a great life with me, but had I a great life with you? I don't know. You're telling me I had, but I don't know that. And if, after 1965, we start to live the life you say we already have lived, will it be the life I want to live? You will then know what is going to happen and I'll be ignorant to it all. And if you know what is going to happen after 1965 and didn't like some of it the last time you'll be able to manipulate things to make sure only what you want to happen happens. After 1965 you will be able to change the things you did not like me doing or saying the last time. You will be in total control of my life. I'll be your puppet to manipulate as you like. Is that not true?"

I was totally unprepared for this reaction from Annette.

"To a degree, I suppose it is," I conceded. "But as you rightly say I have changed all that and given you your life back to live as you wish. And it may not now be the way I remember it was, so in a sense it will be a new life for us both, but one thing I know and one thing that will not change is that I loved you in that life and I want the chance to love you in this one. We can go on from here and disregard meeting in 1965 altogether. We can make this our first meeting and if things turn out as I hope they will our lives will be, I'm sure, just as happy and fulfilling as I remember. And I will never try to change anything you did or might want to do after 1965. It will be a whole new life for both of us."

"Can it really be that? When you met me in 1965 you did not even know my name, is that right? Now you know that and so much more. So right from the start of this or any other relationship between us, how can it be a whole new life when you have the advantage of knowing so much more about me than I know of you? It will not be a coming together of equals, how can it be? Even if you had not come to see me when you found yourself back in 1960 and had waited until 1965, you would still know so much more about me that our future, as you knew it, would or could not be as you remembered living it. You would be able to manipulate things to suit yourself, change the things you did not like in that life and I would not even know what was happening"

I was stunned at the way things were turning around and I was afraid that Annette was going to say she did not want to see me again.

"So," I finally asked with a sigh. "Where does all that leave us? What do we do now? Walk away from each other and pretend this never happened or will you take a chance and see if you can love me?"

I waited for her to reply with trepidation, and after a long period of silence, as we both sized each other up across the table, she said, "We could just go our separate ways now and forget all about this. Forget that it ever happened. I certainly will not be going around telling people I'm a time traveller's wife, and that in some other... world or such like I have a family. That way we both have the chance to live new lives."

"I could not do that Annette," I told her, my eyes filling with tears. "I lost you once and I'm not prepared to lose you again. I love you too much."

She looked across the table and with a searching, penetrating look asked, "What is it you are not telling me? What really happened that caused you to be here?"

I had been determined I was not going to tell her she had passed away in 2009, but I had now got myself into a corner and could see no way out of it. I was about to lose Annette again, if I did not have a convincing reason for being there. I opened my mouth not knowing what was about to come out of it and started to speak.

"Annette, in 2010 I was unfaithful to you, I acted stupidly and I had a one night stand, as such things were called, with another woman. I did not love her, you had been unwell and we had not made love in a long time so one night I was out having a few drinks with a few friends of mine and after drinking too much we got involved with a couple of girls. One thing led to another and I ended up in bed with one of them. I was so ashamed at what I had done that I could not face you and although you had no idea of what I had done the guilt and remorse was too much for me and I told you about the incident. You were unwell at the time and took my admission very badly. You were very hurt and humiliated by my behaviour and it caused your illness to get worse. You had to be hospitalised and you did not want to see me, which caused me to be overcome with such grief and remorse at the hurt I had caused you that I attempted suicide on two occasions. The first time I was saved, but the second time...Well, I really don't know what happened, after taking some pills and whiskey I woke up as the person I am now, in 1960."

I sat waiting for her reaction to the lie, which in truth surprised me, as I did not know what I was going to say when I first opened my mouth and started to speak.

"Andy," she eventually said. "Do you think I'm a complete fool to believe that story? I like you a lot and whether what you are saying about time travelling is true or not, at this point it is immaterial. If it's true you have already changed what will happen between us and if it's not, and it's as phoney as the story you've just told me, you should seriously consider writing novels."

I was caught off guard for a moment and did not know what to say, then she started to laugh and as Annette continued her mischievous laugh, I also laughed and said, "Does that mean I can see you again?"

"I'm not sure that would be a good idea." She was serious again. "Do you really want to play with the future, not knowing what might happen?"

"Why not? Let's toss the crystal balls in the air and see if they break when they hit the ground," I said hoping my levity would entice her to take a chance on me.

She smiled over at me and after a moment of contemplation said, "If it's not as good as you remember it was don't blame me."

I had somehow retrieved the situation and as I reached over across the table and kissed her I said, "It will be even better! Remember the gospel according to Sinatra, "*love is lovelier the second time around.*"

"I really don't know what you're talking about half the time," she replied.

"The future will reveal all," I said and squeezed her hand.

We finished our coffee and as we walked to Aston's Quay to get the last bus to Ballyfermot I was floating on air. This was going to be even better than I had ever imagined it would be. I insisted on going home with Annette and held her tight all the way to her aunt Hannah's house. I knew the bus would be going back to be parked in Conyngham Road Garage for the night as I had so often got it before, after leaving Annette home in another time, so when we got off at the house we stood at the gate and I held her tight until the bus came back down the road a few minutes later.

I then gave her one last lingering kiss, something I had thought I would never do again, before boarding.

Elated at how things had turned out, after thinking I was on the verge of losing her again, I was looking forward to the next four years with Annette.

I had no idea what was going to happen in that time, or now, or even after that – but I didn't care.

Chapter eleven

TO say I was surprised by Annette's reaction to my story of infidelity is putting it mildly.

We met again on Saturday night and we went to see *The Siege Of Sydney Street* which was having its world premier in the Savoy. The film had been shot in Wellington Street the previous year of the last timeframe, just before we moved to the flats in Dominick Street. I had seen the film with my mother and aunts Theresa and Maggie, and it was this thought, as I sat in the Savoy with Annette this time around, that led me to becoming a bit uneasy about changing the course of history – even if in such an insignificant way as attending a film with Annette instead of the people I had attended with last time. I had not told Annette, she did not ask, so maybe she was becoming a bit more relaxed about such things. I was beginning to think that it did not matter anyway. I had now done so much in this timeframe that I had not done before, and it all seemed like the right thing to do, but for some reason I was still a bit uneasy about it.

I was getting what I had prayed for in 2010 but it was not the way I had thought it would be. I cast the doubts out of my mind though and told myself to just be grateful for the chance I had been given. I was with Annette five years before I had met her the first time and that had to be good.

After the show, as we were leaving the cinema, I saw my

mother and aunts in front of us. I was tempted to call to them and introduce Annette, but I did not do so, nor did I point them out to her. I held back until they were well out of the cinema and then turned down O'Connell Street with Annette. Although I knew she had to catch a bus at 11.30pm, and it was now a quarter to the hour, I wanted more time with her. The longer we spent together, I believed, the better my chances were of convincing her our future was together.

As we passed Clerys I impulsively turned to her and said, "Would you like to go to a dance?"

"A dance? Where?"

"Here," I said, "Clerys."

"I have a bus to catch," she said. "We haven't got time."

I took her arm and led her around the corner to Sackville Place, the entrance to the ballroom, saying as I did so, "You're forgetting, my love, that I'm the master of time."

She was too surprised to resist and when we reached the box office I put a pound note on the counter of the ticket kiosk and asked for two tickets.

"How old are you?" the lady in the ticket booth asked as she eyed us up and down, holding the tickets in her hand, having tore them from a roll, which she then replaced under the counter.

"I qualify for the old age pension next year," I truthfully told her and took the tickets from her before she could retract her hand.

"Cheeky," she said and took the pound note off the ledge in front of her before sliding two half crowns towards me. I put the change into my trouser pocket and led a still surprised Annette up the stairs.

After she left her coat in the clothing kiosk we ventured into the ballroom area. The dance was in full swing with couples packing the floor, jiving to the music of an eight-piece dance band.

I took Annette's hand and we pushed our way onto the floor. The band was playing *In The Mood* and I started to jive with Annette, pushing her from me and bringing her back under my raised arm, then doing a full circle as we raised both our arms above our heads and from a back to back position came round to face each other again. As the music ended we wrapped ourselves in each other's arms laughing. Making our way off the floor Annette held my hand and asked, "Where did you learn to dance like that?"

"You taught me. When we met in 1965 I couldn't put one foot in front of the other. You taught me everything I know."

We danced almost every dance until the last one was announced, at which point it suddenly dawned on Annette that she had missed the last bus to Ballyfermot.

"How am I going to get home?" she said in a panic.

"You're not going home. Not yet anyway."

"But, I have to. It's late and the last bus is gone," she said as she fumbled in her bag for the ticket for her coat.

I held her by the hand then and looking into her distressed eyes said, "We're going to one of our favourite restaurants to have something to eat first."

"What!?"

"The Green Rooster. We used to go there after we were married and you liked it a lot."

"I can't, really, it's too late."

"Please, Annette. I don't want this night to end."

"I really enjoyed the night too Andy, but I have to go home now. Mammy and Daddy will be worried sick about me and won't sleep until I'm in."

I could see she meant it so I didn't force the issue, instead saying, "OK. But we'll have to go some other time. I want you to see how well I treated you the last time."

"You're not doing too badly this time," she smiled and kissed me on the face.

We came out of Clerys and I walked her to the taxi rank in the middle of O'Connell Street. Before I put her into a car we kissed, a long lingering kiss, which left the driver agog.

I gave him a pound note after and asked, "Will that get her to Ballyfermot?"

"Just about," he replied and took the money from me.

I told him the address at which to drop Annette, then I looked in at her, sitting contentedly on the back seat and said one word.

"Tomorrow?"

Chapter twelve

MY new found interest in grooming and clean clothes, together with late nights a few times a week, elicited an air of curiosity in my mother, just as my virtual disappearance from the street and football club aroused my friends curiosity. But I was not prepared to let my family or friends know of Annette until I was sure of the situation myself. After the night in Clerys I was more confident of how things would now go between Annette and me. I had been afraid that she was about to end the relationship, but after the way she enjoyed herself and the way she held me close as we danced, I was sure things would be alright and we could now begin to look forward to the future I always knew was ahead of us.

Christmas 1961 was beckoning and we were still together. The Kennedy's had, at this stage, moved into their new home on Le Fanu Road but I had not been there yet. In fact I had not seen Mary and Bill since Newbridge. I usually met Annette at the bus stop on Aston's Quay and we went to the pictures in town or to a "Hop" in one of the new beat clubs that began to open across the city. Last time around I had not frequented these clubs due to my shyness, and awkwardness around girls, but this time, with my very own girlfriend, shyness did not pose a problem and I more than made up for what I missed out on the last time.

I knew Annette loved to dance so I knew I was on a winner when I took her to the beat clubs. The first time I suggested we go to one she was excited, but afraid she would not be allowed in because of her age. She was only fifteen, but I persuaded her to dress in more grown up clothes and with make up on I assured her she would have no trouble passing for eighteen. She had no bother getting in the first time we went to a club, it was me who had to persuade the bouncer that I was old enough to get in.

After the dance in Clerys in October, which proved to be a watershed in our relationship, our dates became more loving and intimate and I began to start thinking that maybe we should not wait until 1965 to begin the relationship proper, as I still thought of it, and start planning for a wedding now.

One chilly afternoon early in the new year of 1962 as we sat in the Palm Grove Cafe I took my courage into my hands and told Annette that I did not think, nor did I want, to wait till 1965 to come out to our friends and families about our relationship. I believed we should do so then, and while not telling them the full story, let them know we were serious about each other and that we were going to get engaged and married. It would be sooner than we had done in the '65 timeframe, but I believed we were ready for it. When I said this Annette remained silent and I held her hand waiting for a reply.

"I'm not sixteen yet," she eventually said, and let go of my hand before touching the ring finger of her left hand.

"I have not even begun to live my life. I work at a job I never wanted, just to please my mother and now you want me to begin living a life you say I have lived before and that I'll be happy living again. Everybody seems to know what I'll be happy with and what's best for me, but all I want is the right and the freedom to live my life as I want to live it. To work at what I want to work at and the choice to marry or not as I so wish. Not to be told what my destiny is. Is that too much to ask or want?"

I tried to hold her hand again but she placed them under the table.

"Annette, love," I pleaded. "I truly want you to be happy and to lead the life you want to lead, but I want to be a part of that life. I want to continue the journey we started in 1965 because I know it was a life you were happy to live. We were both happy to live it and getting the chance to live that life again is something I never thought was possible. But now that we have it I don't want either of us to walk away from it."

Annette took a hankie from her bag and dabbed her eyes. "You're getting the chance to live that life again. I have never lived it. Why can't you be happy the way things are? I've agreed to see you now and not to wait till 1965. If we were married like you say we were, then I know you must be missing the intimacies of marriage and I've tried to make that up to you, can't you be satisfied with that and not want my soul as well as my body?"

"That's just the point," I replied. "We were soulmates the last time around and I want us to enjoy that experience again."

"Andy," she contemplated for a moment. "If we were so close, I … the I… the me, that is still in 2010, why do you not seem to be in the least bit concerned about her? Are you not worried that she is worried about you, about where you have gone? If you were as much in love as you say you were, I…she, must be out of her mind with worry about you. Yet you do not seem to be in the least concerned about that at all. You may be able to travel through time but I doubt that gives you the power to be in two places at the same time. So why are you so unconcerned about her, or me, if we are the same person? If you want me to marry you you'll have to be completely honest with me and tell me the whole truth about how and why you came to be here. I know there is something you are not telling me and unless you are completely honest with me it's unfair of you to just turn up like you did and expect me to believe the things you choose to tell me and to withhold what you don't want to tell me.

She continued, "If you truly did travel from 2010 I want to know the full truth of why you did so, and if we were married then I want to know the full story of our marriage, and the truth about why you are so unconcerned about the wife you say is back in 2010. I want to know the complete truth of how and why you are here now before I make any decision, is that too much to ask?"

I looked across the table at Annette and by her composure I knew I had reached the end of the line. If I wanted this relationship to continue I had to tell her the full truth, now. I had hoped to avoid this, but it seemed now that there was no way we could move on from here unless I was completely honest and truthful with her, and that meant telling her that she had passed away in 2009. I could feel the sweat rolling down my face and under my armpits, as the silence between us became as solid as a concrete wall across the table.

After what seemed an eternity Annette began to stand up saying, "Very well so. If you have nothing else to say on the matter there's no point in my staying here any longer. Goodbye Andy, or whatever your name is."

As she began to move away from the table I reached out my hand to her and held her arm, "No wait" I said, "I'll tell you the truth."

She released herself from my grip, sat back down in the

chair and with a steely look in her eyes said, "The whole truth, everything?"

"Yes," I replied as I took a deep breath, "everything."

Again silence descended as I tried to think of how to start. How to tell her all that had to be said, but in the most delicate and sensitive way possible. How do you tell someone who is sitting in front of you that they are dead?

As Annette waited for me to begin she took a packet of cigarettes from her bag, and still looking at me with a steely determined look lit one before putting the packet back into her bag. She took a long deep pull from the cigarette, held her breath for a moment then carefully and deliberately blew the fusillade of smoke over my shoulder as if she was firing a warning shot across my bows. I inhaled the aroma from the smoke missile as it passed me, and began my story.

"Everything I've told you with the exception of the infidelity bit is the truth. We did meet on August Sunday, 1965 in Bray. We did marry three years later on the 24th of September 1968 and we had three children. David, born on the 19th of June 1970, Gina on the 20th of December 1971 and Robert on the 16th of October 1973. We lived for five years on the North Strand before moving to Tallaght in September 1973 just before Robert was born."

This was going to be harder than I thought, Annette was sitting opposite me scrutinising every word I was saying. To me she was not a sixteen-year-old girl but the mature and intelligent woman whom I had loved for over forty years, and had never, in all that time, been able to fool. I was finding it hard to put the words together and although I knew it was not going to happen I actually expected her to help me out of my predicament, as she used to do when I got myself into awkward situations in our other life.

"Annette," I fumbled on. "We shared a lot of happiness over all those years, but inevitably there was also some sad moments. People passed away, people we both loved, and I'm not sure how much I should say about that. There are things I feel that should be left unsaid, things that I feel you should not know at this stage of our relationship."

Immediately Annette's composure changed and she responded angrily. "Here we go again. You know what's best for me, just like everyone else. If you're not going to tell me everything, only the bits you want me to know, there's no point in you going on or me listening to an edited version of the life I'm supposed to have lived. Do you think I'm so stupid that I would not expect some people to die over a forty year period?"

I reached across the table and tried to take her hand but she pulled it away, so I said, "You're right. You deserve to know the full truth. I just don't know how to tell you."

She calmed down and took another pull from her cigarette before saying, "You've already told me where we met and about you asking daddy for permission to get married, so why don't you start at our wedding? Where was it and who was there? Where did we go for our honeymoon? Start there and we'll see where that leads to."

"Right so." I was feeling a bit more confident now that Annette had, in fact, done what I was hoping she would do,. She had, just like so often in another life, set me on the right course.

"We'll start there so," I said. "That's a good place to start, but we better order some more tea and cakes. It's a long story."

"Better make that coffee," Annette said and took the packet of cigarettes out of her bag again and laid it on the table in front of her, as I called the waitress.

When the waitress brought the coffee I took a sip, replaced the cup on the saucer, took a deep breath and began.

"We were married in the church of the Assumption, in Ballyfermot. It was a Tuesday, chosen because it fitted in with our honeymoon plans to fly to Lloret De Mar in Spain. The weather was really nice, the sun was shining and it was very mild, warm even for late September. You were beautiful in a long white Chiffon over Satin dress, trimmed around the neck with yellow daisies. There were also little daisy's sewn to the body of the dress. You made it yourself. You had a matching long white Chiffon veil, also trimmed with daisies around the part where it sat on your head, and you carried a small bouquet of yellow and white... Carnations I think they were. Your friend Mary Abbey was your bridesmaid and all your sisters, Marie, Claire, Caroline and Louise were Maids of Honour. They were all dressed in long petrol blue Satin dresses that you also made so all that seamstress work in O'Dea's came in handy for something after all. Mary and your sisters carried small bouquets of pink carnations, which you also made, and pink flowers in their hair. You really worked hard on that wedding. My brother Joe was best man and your brother Liam was groomsman."

"What did my mammy wear?" Annette wanted to know.

I had to think for a moment or two before I could recall that it was a Lemon coloured dress and long coat ensemble with a pillbox type lemon coloured hat to match. My mother wore a yellow and brown check suit and a dark brown fur hat I told her. Annette seemed happy with what I was telling her so I continued.

"It was a reasonably small wedding because that's the way we wanted it. We had 52 guests, all family and friends we wanted to be there to share our day with. The reception was held in the Khyber Pass Hotel in Dalkey. A hotel we got to know and you liked when we used to go there sometimes when we were courting. It overlooked Dalkey Island."

Annette broke in at this point and asked, "Did we have any photographs taken of the wedding?"

I smiled as I answered, "Yes, we had lots, and in colour too. It was a great day," I continued. "And everyone enjoyed themselves. There was a slight mishap though, I left our plane tickets, our passports and our money in the wedding car when we got to the hotel in Dalkey and only realised it when it was time for us to leave the hotel for the airport. We had to ring the car hire company. Luckily they found them still in the car and they left them for us in the Gresham Hotel, where we picked them up on our way to the airport that evening."

I could see by Annette's reaction that she was really taking it all in.

"Our honeymoon was ten days in the Santa Rosa Hotel, Lloret De Mar on The Costa Brava in Spain. It was fantastic. Sunshine every day, a rooftop pool and bar and every night we danced until late in the little bars and clubs by the sea front. You even got drunk once or twice on some green coloured mint liquor that you got a taste for."

I became silent for a while then, as my mind travelled back to that time – now so long ago. I relived the magic of it all again, as I had been doing, conjuring it all up in my mind, time after time, since Annette passed away in 2009. It was a whole world away now, maybe more than one world away if what I was experiencing was something that was repeating itself and had done so many times.

"Go on," I heard Annette saying as my reverie was broken and I returned to the present.

I kissed her hand and said, "Will I continue?"

"Yes please," she smiled.

"Very well. When we got back we returned to a small house on the North Strand, which we had bought before we got married, but which needed some renovations. Due to some difficulties with the planning laws it was not ready to be occupied immediately, some work still had to be done on it and your father was helping with that, so while we waited for the work to be completed we rented a bedsit on Mountshannon Road in Rialto."

I suddenly came to a halt then. "Oh by the way you had to leave O'Dea's after you got married, so that's a little bonus for marrying me, something to look forward to if you don't like working there. I can be your escape route."

I tried to make it sound like a joke but Annette just said, "I do like working there. It's just that I would have liked to have a choice about where I worked, the same way as I would like a choice about whether I get married or not."

OK, I thought, *better not go there, just stick to the story,* so I continued and left out the bit I was going to tell her about her getting a job in Ren Tel, the TV rental company, after she left O'Dea's, for fear that she would have told me that she had no intention of working in an office, so I carried on.

"We hated that bedsit and really only slept in it. Luckily we were only in it about four or five months and then early in the new year we moved into our own house in Clinches Court."

I was now coming to a very difficult part of the story and how I was going to tell her I just did not know. If I had some time to prepare and think about it I would have thought of something, but being put on the spot I was totally unprepared. I had promised, however, that I would tell her everything so I had to try and be as delicate as I possibly could be.

During the first year we were in Clinches Court Annette

became pregnant and during that pregnancy her father Bill, became ill and died.

I remained silent for a while but she sat looking at me expectantly. Then when it must have seemed to her that I was not going to continue, she said "Andy, I'm waiting. Are you going to tell me the rest of the story?"

"Can we finish it some other time?" I pleaded. "I think I've told you enough for now."

"Well I don't," she said in a very commanding tone. "You expect me to marry you because you say we were married before in some other time or place and if that is so then I want to know everything about that marriage. Not what you think I should know. If you are not prepared to tell me then you can forget about…"

"You became pregnant," I interrupted her tirade. "You became pregnant after we moved into Clinches Court and…"

"And what?" she demanded. "Go on, I became pregnant and what?"

"Annette it gets very difficult for me here. I do want to tell you everything but there are some things that it would be better if you did not know at this time," I said and hoped beyond hope that she would not press me. But I knew in my heart that there was no way out. She would not be satisfied until she knew everything.

"OK so," she said and stubbed out the cigarette she had been smoking. "If that's all you're prepared to tell me I might as well go home."

I was now feeling desperate and knew that if I did not tell her what happened after she became pregnant it was all over between us and I could kiss goodbye to any chance I had that she would ever marry me.

"Sit down," I said. "I'll tell you everything. We were very

107

happy and very much in love at this time. We both had good jobs, we had a house that we loved and were delighted when you became pregnant. Things could not have been better and we were looking forward so much to the baby which was due in June of 1970. Everything in our world was perfect, there was not a cloud on the horizon."

I did not want to go on, this was not right. I felt I was playing God to some extent, telling her, with complete certainty, that her father was going to die at a particular point in time. Again I pleaded with her not to make me go on, "Annette, please can we stop here? There are some things that it is not necessary for you to know right now. This is not the time or place. If I go on it will only cause you pain and I don't want that. Please don't force me to go on. Take my word for it, there are some things…"

"What happened, did the baby die?" she interrupted.

I remained silent.

"You can't just stop there. Tell me what happened. I want to know, did the baby die?"

I tried to reason with her saying that things may not work out the same way this time and if I continue I may only cause her unnecessary pain, but Annette insisted that I finish what I had started and tell her the whole story. After another period of silence between us, during which I regretted starting this at all, Annette eventually repeated her question, "I want to know, I have a right to know, did the baby die?"

I moved from where I was sitting opposite Annette and went to her side of the table, sat on the chair beside her, put my arm around her shoulder and as I held her tight with my face against her shoulder I said, "No Annette, the baby did not die. This is the second time I will have told you this shocking news, love, and it is not any easier for that. When you were in the early stages of your pregnancy, on our first son David, I had the very difficult job of having to tell you that…that…that your father passed away unexpectedly after a short illness."

There was an audible gasp from Annette and she turned and pushed my head from her shoulder to look at me with in horror.

"What are you saying?" she said choking, trying to hold back the tears I could see welling up in her eyes.

"That's not true. My daddy is not dead. He's alive so he is." I held her close to me, pressing her face into my shoulder to muffle the sound of the distress that was overcoming her and was attracting the attention of other people in the cafe.

"Your daddy is very much alive and will be for years," I told her trying to undo the damage I had done.

Oh God why did it have to be like this? I thought as I remembered the old saying about being careful about what you wished for. After a few moments Annette began to compose herself and she lit another cigarette and asked me to sit back in my own seat, which I did. Nothing was said as we both picked up our cups and drank our coffee and Annette took large pulls from her cigarette as she contemplated what I had said. She eventually dabbed her eyes with a tissue taken from her bag, looked me straight in the eyes and said flatly, "continue the story."

I was now as distressed as I suspected she was, and I did not want to continue. What I was doing was all wrong. I was interfering with time and with events yet to happen, and what effect this would have I did not know. I could visualise what would be likely to happen if we got married in this timeframe and Annette became pregnant. As soon as Bill caught a cold she would insist on the doctor being called and treating him to prevent Pneumonia setting in, and if he recovered and lived, altering the course of history. What would then happen would be unknown to me. Bill's death was a major precursor of events for the whole family and was a major factor in shaping the lives of not only Annette and me but her mother, especially her mother, and the life Mary went on to live after Bill's death. Her sisters and brother would also then go on to lead lives that would be fundamentally different and changed from the way I remembered if Bill continued to live after January 6th 1970. Mary, Liam, Marie and the rest of Annette's siblings, some not even born yet, would go on a trajectory which would be unknown to me if their father was part of their lives as they grew up. If Bill lived it would alter hugely the way all our lives would progress in this timeframe, compared to the one I remembered. Bill's surviving his illness this time and being part of all our lives would alter those lives in a way I had no way of knowing, which in turn would impinge on and alter the lives of all we came in contact with. I had done wrong and I knew it. I had said too much and I did not know how to retrieve the situation.

"I can't go on Annette," I said. "I've already said and done too much damage by telling you what I just have. I have no right to play God and announce when people are going to die. There is no way of knowing the consequences of what I have just told you, but knowing you as I do, I know beyond doubt that if we marry and you become pregnant, if your father develops a cold the first thing you will do is to…

Annette at once interjected and said, "You can't seriously expect me to marry you now? Even if I did so in another "timeframe" as you put it. Daddy's death seems to be all tied up with me marrying you and having a baby. If that does not happen then daddy will not die."

I did not know what to say to that, she seemed to be all

confused, thinking if one thing did not happen then neither would the other. I did not know how to answer so I did not try, I just said, "I don't know what will happen now. I've screwed up everything I was trying to do by telling you what I have. I should not have come to see you at all. I should have waited until 1965 before coming into your life."

Annette gave me a look so withering that I could feel it in my heart and she said, "That's the first thing you've said that makes any sense since I've known you. Yes, you should have waited if you were so certain that we knew each other before and you wanted to see me again, and wanted things to be as you remembered they were. If you were so sure of what had happened, that you had travelled back through time, then you should have waited until 1965 and not jeopardized that life by coming now. Are you so stupid that you did not know that by this course of action you would cause things to be different? Things would have to be different, we're different, both of us are younger. We are not the couple that you say met on Bray Head in 1965. If we ever were that couple we never can be now. And you have caused that. What really caused you to be here now? And don't tell me you don't know, you've just told me when my father will die. If you can tell me that you can tell me anything."

There was no way out for me now I had boxed myself into a corner and I knew it. What I had told Annette was now out of my control. She was right. I had, whether I liked it or not, already changed the course of our lives. Things could never now be as I remembered them. Maybe she was even right about us not being the couple that met on Bray Head in 1965, and if she was, then just who were we?

Things were going in another trajectory altogether thanks to my clumsy attempts to win, again, the affection of Annette. Would it have been better if I had been honest from the start and told her the very first day I got here why I was here? But would a fourteen-year-old school girl have been able to handle someone telling her she was dead in another life and only alive in this one because I had travelled back through time to relive that life with her again?

I had to do something to get out of the predicament. I could not continue along these lines just telling Annette what I felt she was able to cope with. I knew the kind of person she was, or at least had been, and knew she would be more hurt and distressed by hearing of misfortune to others she loved than hearing of misfortune to herself. I was there now and that could not be changed. I also wanted to stay.

Whether Annette decided to marry me or not seemed less important now than putting right what I had done wrong, so I decided to be completely honest with her. Even as I made that decision, though, I was frightened that it would be too much for her. How would she react to hearing that both her father and herself were dead in another time? I reached across the table and took both her hands in mine as I attempted to speak the words that would, I hoped, reassure her that what I had done and said was an honest attempt to protect her from the harsh reality of the truth.

"Annette, I never thought I would be able to do this again, hold your hands and kiss you. I thought that was all over forever, and I would have to live a life of loneliness and emptiness without you, but for whatever reason I've been given a second chance to be with you and I want to do all I can to make it as happy as our last time together. I had thought that it was not necessary for you to know the complete story of our last life, but I can see and understand now that it is necessary for you to know everything about that life if I want you to be my wife again. You are correct in saying I have no right to decide what you should know and what you shouldn't. I have no right to hold back on the things I..."

Here I hesitated as I tried to formulate the words that would sound less shocking and frightening to her.

"Annette you asked me why I'm not concerned or worried about the wife who is back in 2010. The truth is that after a long and happy life together you passed from my life in 2009, taking most of what I was with you. In 2010 I was alone, and living without you."

She released her hands from my grip and irritably said, "What do you mean I passed from your life? What are you trying to say? Say exactly what you mean will you, and don't be talking in riddles."

I again tried to grasp her hands but she kept them under the table as she looked at me with a strange, almost manic, smile on her face and said, "Did I die too? Is that what you're trying to say, that I died?"

Frantically I went to her side of the table again and tried to hold her so as to calm the panic I thought was about to erupt, but she motioned me back to my seat and repeated, "That's it isn't it? I died. You're here to tell me that I died, that I'm dead in 2010."

As she said the words she began to fumble in her bag and took out her rosary beads before blessing herself with them. She was kissing the beads and as she held them to her lips she motioned me to continue.

I was almost as panic-stricken as she appeared to be and I began to cry as I said, "Annette you will never die. Your body may die but your spirit never will. In our past life, after a short illness, you passed away. But very soon after passing into spirit you let me know that you were still very much with me, and even though I knew that, I was still very lonely and missed you terribly. I knew you were in a better place and at peace after the suffering you endured during the illness but that was little consolation in not being able to see you and touch you. Most of all I missed your physical presence in my life, talking to you and walking with you and doing all the little ordinary things we used do. We did everything together and suddenly I was on my own, day and night. I felt only a shadow of the person I used to be. Though I tried to give the impression that I was fine, inside I was dead. As dead as your body, which I had buried. I used go to the cemetery every day and ask you to take me with you. I did not want to be living without you. I believe now that the intensity of my pain and grief and my longing to be with you again, somehow caused me to transcend time and space and come back to you in 1960."

When I finished speaking I looked at Annette. She appeared to be calm now and still holding her rosary beads in her hands asked, "How did I die?"

"Do we have to go into that now? You know why I'm here now. It was not a good time and I don't like remembering it, you were not in any pain and you passed peacefully with all your family around you." I told her through my tears.

Annette then put her beads back into her bag, reached over across the table and gently kissed me on the lips before saying, "It must have been very hard for you, after all those years together finding yourself heading into old age on your own."

This was the Annette I remembered and loved. I had just told her that she had died and her concern was for me. We embraced and I buried my face between her neck and shoulder.

"Come on, let's get out of here," I said as I released myself, conscious of being stared at by the other people in the cafe.

"Where will we go?" She asked.

"Would you like to meet your mother-in-law?"

I smiled and wiped away the tears with a tissue that was on the table.

"My what?!"

I led her from the table then and as we went out of the cafe I turned to Annette and smiling said, "This is going to be a fate worse than death."

Chapter thirteen

THE short walk from the Palm Grove Cafe to Dominick Street was made mostly in silence, both of us no doubt contemplating the strangeness of the situation we found ourselves in.

As we passed Murphy's jewellers on the corner of the Metropole building I tried to lighten the mood by saying, "That's where I bought your 21st birthday present."

"What was it?" she asked without too much enthusiasm.

"You'll have to wait until 1967 to find out." I smiled at her but she didn't react.

Soon we were at the staircase to the flats where we stopped and I held Annette's hand and said to her, "My mother is a good woman and you will get on very well with her over the course of time. You will even come to love her, but she is an Irish mother and she loves her sons and wants the best for them, so don't be nervous if she seems a bit intimidating at first. She'll quickly realise that in you I have got the best. The best that any mother's son could have."

I then kissed Annette on the lips and we climbed the six flights of stairs to the top of the block. I had a key to the hall door, but decided not to use it and knocked. We both stood on the balcony waiting for the door to be opened and we we did Annette looked over it and exclaimed, "Look, you can see Nelson's Pillar from here!"

I smiled, "Yeah, for a few more years at least."

Then the door was opened and my mother was standing in front of us in her trademark, Sunday best, flowery apron. After a moment of surprised silence as she took in the sight of the two of us in front of her she looked at me and asked, "Have you not got your key with you?"

I did not reply to the question, but took Annette's hand and walked past her as she stepped back into the hall looking us both up and down. My father was asleep on a chair beside the boiler that passed for a fire in the living room. He did not wake up when we came in. When my mother came into the room shutting the door to the hall behind her I didn't give her a chance to begin the interrogation I knew she was going to start. I was determined not to have a repeat of the last time she met Annette for the first time so I plunged right in at the deep end and said, "Ma this is Annette, Annette Kennedy, and we might be getting married."

At this announcement both my mother and Annette stared at me with surprised and startled looks on their faces. I just stood, looking back at them and asked, "Why the surprise?"

When the words I had spoken had sunk in my mother said, "You're only seventeen, you can't get married. Is there anything wrong?"

I then told Annette who was still standing, and seemingly too surprised to speak, to sit on the sofa facing the window. I sat beside her, and holding her hand looked up at my mother who was standing looking down at us.

"No, Ma, there's nothing wrong. I've known Annette a long time, a very long time, and I want to marry her. I wanted you and da to meet her, that's all."

At this point my father began to wake up, disturbed, no doubt, by the noise of us talking.

"What's wrong?" he said as he took in the scene in the room.

"There's nothing wrong." my mother answered. "It's only Andrew with his girlfriend."

At this my father woke up fully and said, "His girlfriend? Who's his girlfriend?"

I looked over at him as he tried to understand what was happening and said, "Da, this is Annette, Annette Kennedy, and we might be getting married."

He did not react to what I had just said, nor get up out of the chair but just looked over at us and said to Annette, "Hello, love, how are you? You have lovely hair."

I could not help but smile at this observation because in the previous existence my da had always spoken about and admired Annette's long hair and he was very disappointed when she got it cut. We relaxed a bit then and my mother asked if we would like a cup of tea, to which I said we would and asked if she had any ham left over from the dinner; because I knew that Annette loved my ma's ham the last time and used to love coming up on a Sunday or on holidays when she knew my ma always cooked a piece of ham. Ma confirmed that she had some ham left and went into the kitchen to make some sandwiches and tea. While she was in the kitchen we engaged in small talk with my father who was fascinated by Annette's long hair and wanted to know how she managed to keep it looking so well, he really was taken by her hair. When ma brought out the tea and sandwiches she put them onto the table in the middle of the room and we got up off the couch and sat at it. I handed the plate of ham sandwiches to Annette to take one from and as I did so I smiled at her and said, "You're going to love this, I promise you."

We tucked into the tea and sandwiches and just as I knew

she would, Annette loved hers with *Colman's Mustard*. For the next hour or so we engaged in a conversation about where Annette lived and worked and about her parents and family. Remembering how embarrassed I was the last time Annette and my mother met, because of the way my mother interrogated her, I was determined that this was not going to be a repeat of that occasion; so when ma suggested that she show Annette where the bathroom was I took a firm grip of Annette's arm and led her to the hall telling her the bathroom was to her right at the top of the stairs.

When my mother saw that she was not going to get the chance to be alone with Annette she asked me, "When did you two meet? You never mentioned you were going with a girl."

"It's a long story," I said, "Annette and I go back a long, long way. You could say I've known Annette for a lifetime now."

"That's a strange thing for a seventeen-year-old to say," chipped in my father. "Sure you've both barely started living you're lives."

My mother looked straight into my eyes as if she was trying to read my mind and I averted them from her gaze.

When Annette came down from the bathroom my father commented to her that she seemed to be having a very good effect on me, saying my recent behaviour was becoming very mature and responsible compared to what it used to be and now he knew why.

"Andy's body may only be seventeen, but he has an old head on his shoulders," answered Annette, looking at me smiling.

My mother then said, "I don't know what to make of the pair of you, you seem to be well matched."

"We are," I replied, and gave Annette a kiss on the cheek. "Very well matched."

"The wedding," my mother asked, "When is it?"

"That depends on Annette, when she's ready to get married she'll let me know. It will be when she believes the time is right."

My father then said, "I don't know what it is about you son but for the past while you have not been acting or behaving like any seventeen-year-old I've ever known."

Annette looked at me and smiling said, "I know what you mean. He had a job convincing me he was only seventeen too."

"Come on," I said, thinking the conversation had gone far enough. "We better go or we'll be late for the pictures."

My mother then said to Annette, "If he really has the maturity you like Annette you're very lucky. So don't waste too much time before deciding if you want to get married."

I took Annette's hand and led her to the door as my mother shouted after us, "It was lovely meeting you Annette. Don't be a stranger, come up again."

"She will," I said "you're going to see a lot of her from now on."

"Thanks for the tea," replied Annette. "The ham sandwiches were lovely."

When we got to the bottom of the stairs Annette asked me what picture we were going to see.

"We're not going to the pictures, I just said that so my mother would not monopolise you like she did the first time you met her."

"I thought this was the first time we met, I don't remember meeting her before," Annette replied.

"I do," I said. "And I did not want a repeat of what happened then."

Annette stopped abruptly then and turned to me. "Is this how it's going to be then? You knowing what's going to happen and if you don't like it preventing me from experiencing whatever it is?"

I was lost for words. I had not realised what I had done. I had done it impulsively and without thinking because I wanted to get Annette away from my mother and protect her from the uncomfortable position I knew she would be in if she was left alone with her, but I had, unwittingly, done exactly what I had said I would never do. I had manipulated her life.

"I'm so sorry, love, that's not what I intended at all. I only wanted to protect you from being intimidated by my mother that's all. I can assure you, you would not have liked the experience," was the only excuse I could offer.

I could see Annette was annoyed by my interference and I fully understood her position. I would have felt the same way if the tables were turned and I was the one being "protected."

"Andy, I have not made up my mind yet what to do about our situation, but just when I'm coming around to seeing things from your perspective you do something like this. Despite the fact that you may have lived this life before, I haven't, and I want to be free to live it as I see fit. So if that means being in uncomfortable situations from time to time, or doing things that you don't like, well too bad, but I have a right to travel my own journey and do things my way."

Despite the seriousness of the situation I could not help but smile, as in her outburst I saw the Annette I knew and loved in another life materialise before my very eyes. It was almost exactly word for word what I would have expected the Annette of the 1965 timeframe to have said in a similar situation.

"Do you know what? Sinatra would be proud of you, he could not have done or said it his way any better," I said.

"I don't know what you mean by that," she answered, but I could see that she had got the anger and frustration out of her system and a slight smile was forcing its way across her face.

We started to walk towards O'Connell Street.

"Where are we going?" Annette asked as we came out of the lane and onto Parnell Square. We stopped at the footpath and waited for some cars to pass and as we waited I said, "I don't know, you tell me. Where are we going? The future is now up to you. I'm not going to use my knowledge of what's in that future any more. The way things are panning out now means that I don't know that future anyway, so from here on our future is in your hands. The old template is no longer valid, we have changed our future. You can decide how our relationship develops from here on in. I still want to marry you and hopefully live a life as happy as the one I remember living, but that is now up to you, and whatever you decide I will accept and respect."

This new humble and contrite attitude seemed to catch Annette by surprise and she said, "Can we sit down somewhere and discuss this? So much has happened today I can't really take it all in. I have to clear my head."

"Sure," I said. "Let's go to the Capitol, to the restaurant. The Capitol is the first place we went to together the last time, and this time too, so let's see if we can make this our new beginning."

We continued down O'Connell Street until we came to Princes Street and turned at the GPO. We proceeded past the queue of people waiting to go into the cinema and went up the stairs to the very ornate restaurant on the first floor. We found a table near the wall and sat down and waited to be served by the waitress in her black and white uniform and white headpiece. When she came to take our order, in as authoritative a voice as I could muster, I asked for two glasses of white wine. The waitress hesitated and looked at Annette, but I, as sternly as I could, asked, "Is there a problem?"

The waitress looked at me, her face flushed and said, "No, will that be all?"

I pressed my advantage and replied, "Just two glasses of Chardonnay if you please, and make sure the glasses are cold."

When the waitress went to get our order Annette said, "You should not have ordered wine, I don't drink."

I smiled at her and said, "Annette, love, I know from experience that after two glasses you're anyone's."

She smiled back and replied, "From what you've told me, after two glasses you're no good to anyone."

We both laughed and reached our hands out to each other across the table. It was beginning to feel like it used to, like the times I missed so much when Annette went out of my life, times I thought I would never experience again.

When the waitress came with our drinks we were both laughing loudly with each other. She placed the drinks in front of us, and the bill on a small saucer in the middle of the table. I thanked her and put three shillings on the saucer before handing it to her, intimating that I did not want change. She took the saucer from me and, looking at Annette, blushed and went away. When she had gone I raised my glass and said, "No matter how many lives I live, I hope they are all with you."

She did not say anything in reply but took a sip of wine and after making a face took another sip, then said, "This is not bad at all."

I took a mouthful from my glass, swallowed it and said, "I hope you'll say that after the second time with me."

Then, "Annette I meant what I said earlier, the decision is yours and yours alone. What happens from here on in between us is entirely up to you. I believe the future as I knew it has been changed by what we did tonight, it was not anything like the last time. How you met my parents has changed everything and set us on a completely different course than what I remember."

"Including me dying?" Annette asked, which hit me in the solar plexus as I had almost forgotten our discussion earlier on.

"Maybe," I replied. "Maybe that's why I'm back. Your passing was very unexpected, so much so that maybe it was not meant to happen like it did and I'm back to make sure it does not happen in this timeframe."

"Do you really believe that?" She took another sip of wine.

"Annette before you passed away there was an awful lot I did not believe, but the things that happened after you passed caused me to question very many of my beliefs, and disbeliefs. Now I would not categorically rule out anything – everything and anything is possible. The living proof of that is in front of you. I have lived before in another timeframe or whatever you wish to call it. I am a time traveller. How or why I do not know, but I have come from the year 2010 to be with you. There must be a reason for that, and to make sure you do not pass away as you did the last time round is as good a reason as any I can think of."

Annette did not respond to that, she just took another sip of wine from her glass, replaced it on the table and lit a cigarette before asking so matter-of-factly, "What's it like talking to a dead person? I mean, when you look at me are you thinking, this person is dead?"

I thought for a moment or two before replying, "One thing I learned from your passing the last time is that there is no such thing as death in the accepted sense of that word. Life, or some form of spiritual existence goes on after this phase, of whatever it is we are experiencing now, ends. That's why I always tried not to use the word death or dead when I was referring to you in that previous life. You made that very clear by the things that happened to me after you passed away. Though not physically in my life you continued to let me know you were still around in some shape or form, so when I look at and talk to you now I don't think of you as dead. I focus on how lucky I am to be given the chance to spend another life time with the person I love."

"What kind of things happened?" Annette asked.

"I really don't know how to describe them or speak of them, but I'll just say that things, that at first I thought were coincidences, started to happen and when these coincidences kept happening I began to believe that they were not really coincidences, but that you were communicating with me from wherever you had passed over to. That's all I can say about it as I don't really understand it myself. I suppose it really comes down to believing there is more to life and death than we can know about, or understand in one lifetime."

I hoped she would not press me to tell her more.

"Did you hear my voice after I died?" she wanted to know.

"Yes," I replied. "Every day, though not a ghostly voice. I heard it on your CD, which I played every morning after getting up."

"What's a CD?"

"Sorry," I laughed "I should have mentioned it before, but I did not want you telling it to Willie Rogers or he might have stuck with you and had you working for him and giving him your compositions. A Compact Disc or CD for short, is something that will be invented in the future. It's like a

125

record only much smaller in size, and capable of holding a lot more music or dialogue. You started to compose songs after we were married, very good songs too they were, and when you had a few pounds you hired a studio and recorded them onto a CD. Anyway I had that CD and I played it every day after you passed away, just so I could hear the sound of your voice in the house."

"Sing me one of my songs," Annette asked with excitement.

"No, I'll never do that. You'll compose them in the future. If I sang them for you now you would not be able to claim them as your songs because you would have heard them before. So no, Annette, that's one thing I'll never do."

The wine seemed to have affected Annette as I noticed she was beginning to slur her words slightly and was talking in a more animated way than previously. She swallowed the last of what was in her glass and in a somewhat loud voice said, "Do you know what, that was nicer than I expected, I think I'll have another glass of wine."

I thought it better not to get her anymore as it was affecting her in a way I had not expected, so I looked at my watch and said, "It's getting late, I think we'd better go in case we miss the last bus. I'll get you another glass of wine the next time we're out."

"I was really enjoying that, do we have to go?"

"I think we'd better." I began to stand up.

"Well if you won't sing one of my songs or get me another glass of wine will you at least tell me where you buried me when I died?" She said this in a voice loud enough to be heard a few tables away, which caused some people to turn and look at us. It really was time to go, so I stepped to her side of the table and handed her coat to her before leading her out of the restaurant.

"Do we have to go?" she asked again. "I was really enjoying

our little chat."

"We better," I said. "It's late. It's after eleven. I'll leave you home and we can talk again tomorrow."

"Ok, I'm getting tired anyway, but you have to tell me where you buried me, do you hear?"

The people sitting at the next table turned their heads again as we made our way past them.

"I'll tell you tomorrow," I said and helped her put her coat on.

Annette clung to me as we headed down to the quays for the bus to Ballyfermot. I was hoping she would be sober before we got home. I had not met Mary and Bill since the day in Newbridge and I did not want them to think I was a bad influence on their underage daughter, getting her drunk. Luckily we had to wait a while for the bus in the cold air on the quays and this gave Annette a chance to sober up and become alert before she got home.

By the time we reached the corner of Le Fanu Road and walked up to her house she was OK again. I did not go into the house with her but kissed her at her gate and said I would see her tomorrow, to which she said a sleepy, "OK."

Chapter fourteen

WHEN I got home that night my mother was still up. She was sitting at the fire having a cup of tea before going to bed. My father was already in bed, as was Joe.

When I came into the room my mother seemed to be deep in thought and when I commented on her still being up she looked at me in a way I had never seen before – a way which implied to me that she was troubled about something.

Then she said, "You're a dark horse, where did you meet her?"

"Bray," I told her and went into the kitchen to get a cup of tea and a sandwich.

"What were you doing in Bray in the middle of winter?" she called into me, as I stood beside the cooker and lit the gas under the kettle.

"It was a long time ago, in the summer," I replied.

"And you never mentioned her until now?"

"The time was not right."

I came out of the kitchen and sat at the table in the living room.

"She seems like a nice girl."

"She is, there's no one nicer." "

"Are you serious about getting married?" Her eyes were penetrating.

"Yes!"

"But you're both very young. How old is Annette?"

"Age does not matter, I love her."

I said surprising myself, being so forthright.

"Does she love you?"

I could not answer that as I did not know, or rather I did know, but I did not want to answer it now, preferring to believe that she would, given time, so I blustered an answer.

"She would not be with me if she didn't." I said, more to convince myself than my mother. "Don't worry about that, everything will be alright, I know it will."

"Marriage is forever," my mother said "and it's not always a bed of roses. Things don't stay the way they were when the courting ends and the serious business of building a life together begins after the honeymoon. People change over the years and getting married young means you will have a lot more years ahead of you, a lot more years to change."

I never heard my mother speak like this in the past, she seemed like a different woman to the one I remembered. I looked at her as she was saying this and I could see a wistful look on her face, a look of longing for something lost. Then, coming out of her reverie, she stood up and brought her cup into the kitchen as she said, "Ah sure everyone's life is different and no one knows what's ahead of any of us. Maybe getting married young means you can grow up together and have a longer time to get over your mistakes. Don't stay up too late, I'm tired, I'm going up to my bed of roses."

I smiled at her and said, "Goodnight, Ma. See you in the morning."

This was the first time since I was back that I'd had a serious conversation with either of my parents, short and all as it was. Up to this I had been just rushing in and out, going to work and seeing Annette. I sat for a while thinking about what she had said and the way she had said it. This woman did not sound or behave like the mother I knew in my past life, she was much more philosophical and open in her manner of speaking, which set me thinking if I should mention anything about my situation to her... or was that a bridge too far, something beyond her comprehension?

No one other than Annette was aware of my strange predicament and she had not even mentioned it to her parents, of that I was sure. I thought long and hard about it after my mother went to bed, but in the end I decided not to say anything, at least not yet. The secret would remain between Annette and me for the time being. So I had my cup of tea and went to bed.

When I went to work the next day, after our discussion in the Capitol Restaurant, I received a phone call from Annette just before lunch. She did not want to see me again, she was distressed about me telling her that she had died in another life and she explained that being with me would be a constant reminder to her of what was to come. She knew everyone had to die at some time, but being with me, she said, would be like counting down the days to her death. It would be like waiting for a time bomb to explode or her head on the guillotine waiting for the blade to fall. I was devastated and tried to reason with her, saying that it need not necessarily be the same this time but her mind was made up, we were through and she wanted to lead her life without me.

I knew I should not have told her about her death, it was too much for her to have to absorb and live with. She was, after all, only a young girl and I was speaking to her as if she was the mature adult I had known in another life. I pleaded with her to reconsider and to see me at least one more time, to give me the chance to try and put things right, but she was adamant and as I pleaded she hung up on me.

I had said that I would respect her decision about our future, no matter what it was, but now that she had made her mind up I just could not accept it and live up to the noble words I had spoken to her.

I was in shock, things had seemed to be going so well between us and I had thought she had handled the news about her death very well, made light of it even by wanting to know where she had been buried. But now this. It was like a bombshell and I just could not handle it. My mind was in turmoil and I just did not know what to do or who to turn to. I had, in fact, no one to turn to. Annette was the person I would have looked to for advice at a time like this, but it was Annette who had caused my predicament.

I did not say anything to anyone about Annette breaking up with me and after a few evenings of silent teas, and nights spent in my room indulging my depression by listening to Sinatra at his melancholic best, my mother came up the stairs and called me, "Andrew are you alright, what's wrong? Are you not going out with Annette tonight?"

I did not open the door but answered her by saying, "I'm alright, I'm not going out tonight."

"Is everything alright between Annette and you? Did you have a falling out or something?"

I did not answer her, but turned the volume up on the record player. Then the door opened and she stepped into the room.

"What's wrong?" She looked at me lying on the bed with my eyes tightly shut. I did not respond.

"There's something wrong, what is it? There wasn't a word out of you at the tea and you haven't been yourself this past while. Is it something to do with Annette. Is she alright, she's not..."

"Oh, Ma," I interjected, irritated now by her persistence. "There's nothing wrong. Annette is not pregnant if that's what you're thinking."

"Then what is it? You've changed this past while. I've noticed a lot of changes in you, in your behaviour and your attitude, it's as if…as if you're a different person."

"I don't want to talk about it, you would not understand."

"Then something did happen?" she persisted.

"Annette happened, that's all. Now will you please leave me alone?"

"Very well," she said and turned to go out of the room, but not before adding "Everyone has rows, it's part of life, you'll just have to get over it."

"We didn't have a row," I said. "She just wants a bit of time to think about things."

As my mother stood at the door she said, "You're both very young, you should do a bit of thinking too, and even if you do break up with Annette, just remember, time is a great healer."

I turned on my back and smiled at what she had said. If only she knew the wound time had opened up – it would take a very long time before it would even begin to heal.

So, that seemed to be the end of the relationship, my journey through time was a waste of it apparently. Annette had rejected me and I was now, it seemed, going to be forced to live my life all over again without the woman I loved by my side. Now I really did not know what the future held for me as all the things I remembered, all the things that were good about my past life, Annette had been a huge part of, but now she was gone and I had to forge a new life.

What my future, without her in it, was going to be I had no idea. I had no interest or desire in forming another relationship with anyone else. I loved Annette and it was her I wanted and only her. The idea of being with someone else was repugnant to me and, likewise, the idea of Annette being with anyone but me was agony to think of.

I did not contact or try to see Annette after the phone call. I had said that I would respect her decision and that's what I did, but it was hard. She was on my mind all the time and I could not motivate myself to do anything. I was lethargic and irritable at the same time. I withdrew from, and was not communicating with my family, particularly with my mother who from time to time asked me about Annette and whether I had been in contact with her. I just shrugged all her entreaties away and told her that was all over and to forget it as I had. Deep inside, though, I knew, she knew that was not true.

I lacked interest in almost everything at the time and I even became very careless about my work situation, sleeping late, missing days and losing and moving through a succession of dead-end jobs, because it seemed to me I had no good reason to bother working anymore – without Annette in my life there was nothing to work for. All this behaviour was a cause of friction at home but I did not care anymore. I was beyond caring what anyone thought now. The only thing I had the slightest bit of interest in was sport, and most Sunday afternoons I found a bit of relief and a refuge for my miseries by going to Milltown to see Paddy Coad and his colts beat the shit out of most teams they played. That's what kept me from losing everything, maybe even my life.

I was still a member of the football club, although I had not played nor made myself available to them very often in the previous year or so. Just for something to do, however, and to get out of the flat and away from my mother's probing questions, I resumed training in the clubhouse on Tuesday and Thursday nights; and very soon I was back in the team having resumed my friendship with Anthony Williams and Damien Murphy. We had been close friends the first time around, and it was easy picking up the pieces again.

After being back playing football for a while I did relax a little and tried to behave as any normal seventeen-year-old would. I suppose the fact that I had experienced the pleasure of female company made me want to indulge in that past time again, though in truth I knew that it would be a futile exercise as I could never imagine myself forming a relationship with anyone because Annette would always be such a huge part of what I was. The last time around we did not go in much for chasing girls or drinking, preferring football, the cinema and Sunday nights at the Theatre Royal to dance halls and pubs – but this time I, after a while, became very much the leader of the pack and began to encourage a healthy interest in the opposite sex and in pushing our luck in trying to get served in pubs.

At first I was a bit concerned about doing this as I did not want, in any way, to alter the course of my friends lives and be responsible for them marrying anyone other than the girls I knew they would marry, but I rationalised my actions by telling myself that things were already changed from the way I remembered and that maybe destiny had a different life plan for all of us this time. Anyway, they soon lost their shyness and participated fully, with no help from me, in pulling girls and downing pints.

Although it was me who had encouraged and led the charge for female companionship the novelty soon wore thin for me and I gradually withdrew from the nights in the pubs and the dance halls. I just could not form a relationship with anyone, and I was being most unfair to the girls I did, from time to time, date by comparing them to Annette and, always, there was no comparison. There was also the added burden that I always felt in that by being with another girl I was cheating on the one I loved, and that was one thing I was not prepared to do. Even though Annette had made it clear that she was not going to resume our relationship my love for her was unconditional.

After my withdrawal from the social side of the friendship with the lads I did continue to train and play football every week and I did occasionally go to a dance on my own. The Macushla Ballroom near Amiens Street station was a hall that I knew Annette used to frequent from our conversations in the '65 timeframe, and in the hope of seeing her I went there once or twice, but I never did see her and usually went home alone, crestfallen. I also went on bus trips to places Annette and I used to go to, like Glendalough and Dalkey and I even got the bus to Tallaght one day and had a look at where we lived in the 1965 timeframe, but Raheen Green was only an open field off the narrow Old Blessington Road – way out in the country with not a house nor a person in sight.

I did find it fascinating to be seeing Dublin in its pre-developed state, knowing what was coming down the road very soon. But all this activity on my part was only a means of trying to kill time until 1965 came around again. A time when I knew I would be going to Bray. I was hoping beyond hope that by then Annette would be curious enough to want know if I still wanted history, or whatever this was, to repeat itself, and do the same.

Despite everything I had not given up hope that our paths would converge again sometime in the future, in fact I was sure they would, and this belief is what kept me going. I knew Annette so well and I was certain that over the course of time, as she got older, she would reassess all the things

I had told her and with that knowledge and the belief that I was sincere in my motives that she might reverse her decision. I knew Annette was still working in O'Dea's and from time to time I was sorely tempted to try and see her again, but I resisted.

I did not drive in the '65 timeframe, partly because I was not interested in cars or any other type of technology for that matter, I preferred my trusty bike and public transport for getting me around. The Internet, computers iPhones and games left me stone cold and I never had any interest in the social networks, then all the rage.

Another reason for my not driving then was the fact that for most of the time I did not have the money to buy a car, but this time money, at least, was not a great problem. I still had no great interest in cars, they were just a means of getting from one place to another as far as I was concerned, but I knew that if I ever got back with Annette, which I was sure I would, that she liked to travel and if I had a car it would be to my advantage as I would be able to bring her to all the places I knew she liked. So, planning ahead so to speak, I placed an accumulator bet on Dundalk winning the League of Ireland and Shelbourne winning the FAI Cup of season '62/'63 as well as Tipperary and Kerry winning the hurling and football All-Ireland Finals of 1963 – a bet I knew I could not lose. I did not like doing this and did not do it very often, and even when I did I only bet a modest amount, enough to get me what I wanted at any particular time. This time I wanted a car, not necessarily a new car but one that would impress Annette. I rationalised my behaviour by setting it alongside my future with Annette and felt justified in doing this because if we did get back together I was determined to use every means at my disposal to make sure it would be permanent.

When all the results were confirmed in late September I collected my winnings and bought myself an old blue Austin Cambridge car.

My uncle Tom, my mother's brother, who was the proud owner of an old Morris Minor taught me to drive in his own inimitable way on roads that seemed, compared to what I remembered from 2010, to be almost devoid of traffic, but certanly not as good. I confined my driving to up and down the main road of the Phoenix Park until I got used to handling the car, and then one Saturday morning I decided to go further and headed out the Chapelizod gate and up towards Ballyfermot. When I got to the corner of Ballyfermot and Kylemore Roads I passed the church where we were married in 1968 and crossed the roundabout, continued down Kylemore Road and turned up Kylemore Avenue towards Le Fanu Road.

I stopped on the corner, knowing that if I turned left I would be very near Annette's house, very near Annette. After a few moments of confused uncertainty I turned the key in the ignition and with a screech of tyres I turned and headed back down Le Fanu Road and home.

It was a very lonely and confused time for me now without Annette and I did not allow the friendship with Anthony and Damien to develop as it had done in the previous time. We were drinking more this time too and I was conscious that this was not a good thing to be doing as I felt it was very likely that some night, if I was feeling depressed or morose and under the influence of too much drink, I was very likely to blurt out something that I'd be sorry for. It was painful trying to come to terms with the fact that I had lost Annette again but I knew even as I was doing so that drinking too much was not the answer to my situation.

After Annette passed out of my life the last time I had

hoped and prayed, which was not an easy or practical thing for someone such as I, who had never had any faith in prayer or religion, for the chance to be with her again.

I got that chance, and then I lost it. I didn't know where to go from there.

I was sorry I had acted with such haste in letting her know I was back when she had not even known I was gone. But the damage was done and I was not sure if it could be undone. I knew for certain that I had to resist all temptation and not contact her again, and when August Sunday 1965 came around I hoped she would still remember me and be curious enough to go to Bray – right now that seemed like a very forlorn hope, but it was all I had to cling to.

And if that's what it took then for the next two years I would not attempt to see Annette, though I would dearly have loved to experience some of the historic events of the next couple of years with her.

Chapter fifteen

SUDDENLY November the 7th, 1963 was here again and I was back in the Adelphi Cinema to see The Beatles.

Just like the last time I was with my friends Anthony and Damien, but this time we had female company. The Beatles and their music were proving to be just as popular this time around and when it was announced that they were coming to Ireland I asked Anthony and Damien, whom I was still playing football with, though not socialising with as often as before, if they were interested in going to see them.

As I had not been socialising with them on a regular basis I was unaware that both of them were now in relationships with girls. Since it was me who had encouraged this interest I had no reason to be surprised, but when this was pointed out to me I was a bit embarrassed as I felt that I was encroaching on their newfound relationships. I was not involved with anyone at this time and I thought that they would think I was only using them when I wanted companionship to go to some event or other.

One of them suggested that I should ask some girl to go with me and we could all go together. This was something I had not expected. I was not in the least interested, at that time, in getting involved with anyone other than Annette, and I had ruled out any contact with her until 1965. Anyway I knew what her answer would be if I did get in contact with her – the same as it had been when I asked her to come to see Adam Faith in 1960. I would have to think long and hard before I would consider asking anyone to come to The Beatles concert with me, but I had seen The Beatles with Anthony and Damien the last time around and it felt only right to me that we should see them together this time too.

Damien suggested that there was plenty of girls to choose from if I wanted a companion as the youth club, which had previously been an all boys club but had recently opened its membership to the fairer sex – the arrival of whom had done wonders for the morale and personal hygiene of the lads. I must say that I was, or at least could have been, attracted to one or two of the new arrivals if Annette had not been on my mind so much. I knew that Anthony had met his future wife Rita Power, when she joined the club, but he had not started to go out with her in this timeframe yet.

I had always liked and got on well with Rita previously and even now I found her to be a very nice person and someone I found it easy to talk to when we would have a chat in the club. But knowing what I did I never encouraged anything further than platonic friendship. I considered what Damien had suggested though, and knowing that the date would not lead to anything romantically I decided to ask Rita if she would be interested in coming to the concert with me, explaining to her the fact that we would be with Anthony and Damien and their girlfriends. She readily agreed and I, without mentioning who I had asked, told Anthony and Damien that I had a date to go to the show with, and a month before The Beatles arrived in Ireland the three of us queued for over two hours one Saturday morning, in a line that stretched from the Adelphi all the way up Abbey Street and around the corner into O'Connell Street, to get tickets for the nine o'clock show on Thursday, the 7th of November, 1963.

The tickets cost six shillings and six pence each. After getting them we went to the Pillar cafe for a cup of coffee and over the course of the conversation decided that as our girlfriends had never met each other it might be a good idea to go out together before the concert, so they could get acquainted with each other and us with them. I still had not said who I was bringing, only mentioning that I had asked a girl out of the club and when Damien said he was glad and asked me who it was, I felt a pang of guilt as I looked at Anthony and said, "Rita, I asked Rita Power."

Immediately Anthony responded by saying in a surprised voice, "Rita Power, out of the club?"

"Yes," I said. "I asked Rita and she is delighted to be coming, so at least you both know her."

"Have you been out with her before?" Anthony then asked me.

"No. I'm not with anyone at the moment. When Damien suggested I ask someone out of the club I just asked Rita as I had often spoken to her before and we seemed to get on well, that's all."

Then mischievously, "Why are you so interested in Rita?"

"I'm not," he blustered and his face went red. "Are you going out with her before The Beatles show?"

"I had no plans to, but now that it's been decided that we should all get acquainted before the show I'll ask her if she would like to come too," I replied as calmly and as disinterestedly as I could, while trying to keep a straight face.

"She's a nice looking girl, you did well there," Anthony responded.

"Yeah, she is that," I said with a big grin on my face. "She'll make someone a lovely wife someday."

Before we left the cafe it was agreed that we would all meet again on Saturday, the 26th of October, which was less than two weeks before The Beatles concert and we would go somewhere for a drink and a chat where the girls could get to know each other.

I would previously only go to the club for training on Tuesday and Thursday nights and leave immediately after, I did not participate in the social interaction that had started to develop between the boys and girls since the club became unisex; but on the Tuesday night before we were all due to meet I stayed behind to see Rita and ask her if she would like to come out with me. She said that she would love to do that and as we were talking I noticed Anthony taking a great interest in us. I called him over and it transpired that although he knew who Rita was he had never, up to then, spoken to her.

You know how it is when you're attracted to someone, you put them on a pedestal and feel unworthy to approach them, so I did the introductions and marvelled at the ways of the world. Here I was back in 1963, on my second life, introducing my friend to the girl he had married in a previous existence. After making arrangements to meet Rita on the Saturday night I excused myself and left Anthony and her talking, neither of them seeming too concerned that I was leaving. I stood at the door of the hall and looked back at the two of them, engrossed in conversation and seeming as if they had been friends all their lives. I could not help smiling to myself.

On the Saturday we were all due to meet Damien could not make it, so obviously we did not get to meet his girlfriend. Anthony and I were now gone eighteen and legally entitled to enter a pub and have a drink, which we were known to do from time to time, but our girlfriends were not yet quite old enough to legally buy alcohol.

I did not bring my newly acquired car that night as we intended staying in town and had arranged to meet at the Pillar as it was convenient for us all. I was living in Dominick Street, Anthony was also living in town and Rita was living in Phibsborough, but although I had offered to pick her up she said she would get the bus into town. Anthony's girlfriend, whom I had not met, was living in Cuffe Street. I called for Anthony and we walked to the Pillar together. On the way down he remarked to me, rather enviously I thought, how lucky I was to have Rita for my date. He told me about the long conversation he had with her on Tuesday night and how he thought she was a really nice and attractive girl. He also joked that he wished he'd got there before me.

I just smiled and said, "Really? Well if you want something you just have to go for it."

It was not long before Helen, Anthony's date, came along. She could not have been more different from Rita. She was almost eighteen, of short stocky build with obviously dyed jet-black hair piled high on her head to give her extra height, a heavily made up face and a figure not designed for the black mini skirt and tight red polo-necked sweater she was wearing under a fake leopard print short plastic jacket. She came into view hobbling along on red high-heeled shoes that she was in danger of falling off and as Anthony introduced her to me I was amazed that I had been so far off the mark when trying to visualise the type of girl he would date before he started going out with Rita.

Having said that, Helen, despite her appearance was a very nice girl and after the initial shock I tended not to take too much notice of her appearance as her personality took over. We stood talking for a while as we waited for Rita and after a few minutes Helen remarked that she was getting cold and hoped that my date was worth waiting for. Before I could respond to her Anthony interjected and said, "Here she comes now and she's looking great. Well worth waiting for."

Helen poked him in the ribs and remarked that she was his date and not to forget it. Rita made her way across the road from her bus stop and the contrast between the two girls could not have been more obvious. Rita was at least three inches taller than Helen with her hair naturally dark and cut short, styled to look like a hood over her head. She was wearing a calf-length deep red coat with a black satin trim down the front and around the sleeves, and medium height black leather shoes. She was also carrying a small black shoulder bag. After more introductions we all headed over to the Metropole bar. Inside we found a table for four and myself and Anthony ordered a pint of *Celebration* ale each while the girls opted for dressed orange juice. After one or two more pints and a glass of wine for each of the girls we began to relax and enjoy the surroundings. I had been in the Metropole a few times in my previous life but this was the first time in this existence, and I tried to remember if the decor was the same.

The girls, despite their radically different dress style, got on very well until Anthony, after few more pints began to pay more attention to Rita than he should have done. In another situation or context I would have been annoyed, but knowing their future history I felt I was the one out of order, after all Rita was going to be his wife in a few years time. Nevertheless I was conscious that both Rita and Helen were uncomfortable with the situation and tried to steer the conversation towards the upcoming concert.

I remembered it well, and without giving too much away,

I got their attention for a while by telling them what I thought it would be like, citing reports from newspapers and magazines and speculating on how big The Beatles would be. This only held Anthony's attention for a while and soon he was trying to monopolise Rita again, at which point Helen said she was tired and wanted to go home.

I looked at my watch, it was after 11pm and the night had gone on long enough, so before irreparable damage was caused I looked at Rita, who I could tell was uncomfortable, and asked her if she was ready to go. She seemed relieved that the night was almost over and was happy to confirm that she was ready to leave. I helped her on with her coat while at the same time noticing that Helen declined Anthony's help in putting on hers. We checked that we were not leaving anything behind and left the bar in silence. Outside, under the canopy, we said a somewhat embarrassed goodnight and went in different directions – Anthony and Helen walking down towards O'Connell Bridge and Rita and me walking up to get the bus outside the Carlton Cinema.

As we walked up O'Connell Street there was an uneasy silence between us and I did not attempt to hold Rita's hand as I would have done had I been with any other girl, especially Annette. When we got to the bus stop there was a small queue and as we stood waiting for the bus Rita remarked on Anthony's behaviour and said that she had felt embarrassed by the way he was ignoring Helen and paying so much attention to her. I told her not to judge Anthony on what happened tonight as he really was a nice guy and was not normally so rude. I excused his behaviour by saying that he did not usually drink as much as he had done. Rita replied that she was surprised by his conduct and the way he had acted as what she knew of him from the club had led her to believe he was a well mannered person, and although she had only spoken to him for the first time last week she thought then that he was a very nice boy.

I again told her that tonight was an exception and not to form an opinion of him based on one incident. "We're all prone to do stupid things from time to time," I said.

Especially when you fancy someone big time I thought to myself.

When the bus came and the queue of people began to get on Rita said that I did not have to go home with her. She insisted that she would be alright as the bus stopped almost outside her door. I was relieved and glad of that as I did not want to be put in a position where she or I would feel that the night would have to end with a kiss and an embrace, something I didn't think I would have been able to handle. So I guided her onto the bus and as she went upstairs we just waved to each other. I said I would see her in the club before The Beatles concert.

When the bus pulled away I stood for a while and watched as the cinemas emptied of patrons and fresh bus queues were formed by the ghosts of my past life.

I walked away from the bus stop and turned the corner at the old Hibernian Bank then went into Mooney's pub in Parnell Street for a final pint before closing time was called.

I sat in a corner of the pub and contemplated the evening's events. Despite Anthony's behaviour it had been an enjoyable, if somewhat strange, night. A night that had not occurred the last time around and I wondered what other twists and surprises this life had in store for me, before Annette and I met again and hopefully embarked on the life I thought I knew so well.

Chapter sixteen

I ONLY saw Rita once before the night of The Beatles concert and that was in the club when I went training on the Tuesday before the show. I stayed back afterwards to make arrangements with her to pick her up on the Thursday night. Nothing was said about the night in the Metropole, but before I left, which I did immediately after speaking to Rita, I noticed Anthony hanging back and then talking to her when I left her company. It seemed like he was taking my advice about going for the something he really wanted! I did not mind in the least as I was intent on getting back with Annette and so both of us would hopefully get the girl of our dreams.

The night of the concert finally arrived and I drove to Phibsborough to pick Rita up from her house. I did not go inside but waited in the car. A moment or two after arriving I noticed the curtain being opened and Rita looked out of the window. I hit the horn twice and she waved to me before coming out the hall door and walking down the short garden path. She was wearing the same coat she had worn the night we went to the Metropole. It was not buttoned and as she walked to the car and I could see she had a dark red skirt with a navy waistband and a brownish coloured top. She was not carrying a bag, she had instead a small black patent purse and a scarf in her hand. I leaned over and opened the car door for her. I made no effort to be over familiar or kiss her, I just smiled and said, "Are you ready to experience something never before seen in Ireland?"

"Do you think it will be that good?" she replied.

"It will, and the show will be great too," I laughed.

She just looked at me and I smiled a knowing smile and said, "Just wait and see."

I drove back to the flats and parked the car in Granby Lane and we walked to Easons on O'Connell Street where we were to meet Anthony and Damien and their girls at about 8.15pm. They were there when we arrived and I was somewhat surprised to see that Damien was not with Joyce, the girl he married the last time, but with another girl I remembered him being with previously. Patricia Nolan was a dark haired, surly, stout girl who had not liked me very much the last time, and by the manner of her greeting did not care too much for me now either.

Helen, I observed was more conservatively dressed this time in a longer skirt and a dark-belted wool coat. Her hair was more carefully groomed than the last time as well. She was rather quiet in her greeting, no doubt the last outing was still rankling with her. After a few words about the night in store I suggested that we made our way to the cinema. I knew what to expect and so I wanted to get there early. I wanted to experience, once more, one of the wildest nights Dublin had ever seen.

We could hear the commotion in Abbey Street even before we turned the corner from Easons. It was pandemonium. The street was jammed tight with people stretching from the offices of the Irish Independent to the entrance to the Adelphi, half of them wanting to get into the cinema, half of them wanting to get out after seeing the 6.30pm show. Many more were just standing in front of the cinema and screaming for a glimpse of The Beatles.

I knew we had no chance of forcing our way through the throng, with the girls in tow, as we had done the last time when we were on our own. So when we had taken a good look at the scene I suggested that we go back up O'Connell Street and make our way down Princes Street and approach the Adelphi from Williams Lane, which would bring us up ahead of most of the crowd and very near the entrance to the cinema. That way we would not have to battle our way through the crowds the length of Abbey Street. This we did, and with the assistance of a Garda who was on duty at the end of Williams Lane, to whom we showed our tickets, we very soon found ourselves at the front of the Adelphi, behind a cordon of bewildered Gardai who were endeavouring to only admit those with tickets through their ranks. When we were safely at the doors of the Adelphi I turned to a shocked and open-mouthed Rita and asked, "Well, what did I tell you?"

When we eventually got into the cinema the noise was even louder than outside, and the show had not even started. We found six empty seats a little more than half way up the auditorium and occupied them. Whether they were our seats or not I was not sure, as people, mostly young girls were running wild all around the cinema trying to get as near to the stage as they possibly could. Some of them were hanging over the pit wall in front of the stage as ushers tried, in vain, to drag them back for fear that they would fall into the pit if they tried to get onto the stage.

From the balcony above us girls were just hanging over the front screaming. It was impossible to talk with all the noise so we just sat and observed the wonderful mayhem reigning all around us and waited for the show to start.

I truly enjoyed the privilege of seeing it all again, probably more than I had the first time, and watching the reaction of those experiencing "Beatlemania" for the first time was an exhilarating feeling.

After about fifteen minutes the house lights were dimmed and if we thought the place had been noisy up to then, we we were mistaken. The cinema was now in darkness, apart from the lights illuminating the magnificent gold-coloured stage curtains embroidered with multi-coloured butterflies, and the audience was now in full voice. As the curtains began to part, the noise got even louder and I don't think one single person in the cinema was sitting in their seat – everyone was on their feet screaming at the top of their voice. The support acts, which included The Vernon Girls, The Kestrels, Peter Jay and The Jaywalker's and Sounds Incorporated – whose drummer had a drum kit set up so that every time he hit it the drums lit up. The support was very good, but nobody wanted to hear them. They played their sets to a constant refrain of, *We Want The Beatles, We Want The Beatles!*

When compere, Frank Berry, finally announced the main act, what had passed for noise up to then seemed like the gentle rustling of leaves being blown by the wind – it was incredible. I did not think it was possible for the human voice to make such a sound. The walls of the cinema seemed to buckle as the wave of hysteria hit them and then like a sling, cast the noise back into the ears of those making it.

Just like the first time I saw The Beatles it was impossible to hear what they were singing. From the moment they opened their set with, *When I Saw Her Standing There,* until their closing number, *She Loves You Yeah Yeah Yeah,* I don't think anyone in the cinema could have possibly heard more than a dozen words.

It was a truly amazing experience to be sitting in the

Adelphi again as history repeated itself, well at least for me. Seeing The Beatles appearing on the stage, in what became their trademark silver gray suits with no collars and pointy Beatle boots, with Ringo sitting on a raised podium behind his big drum kit, was a magical experience. And despite everything I was feeling about Annette not being in my life, for an hour or two at least, I felt happy again.

Then suddenly it was all over and as the safety curtain came down between the band and their devoted fans the audience again took up the chant, *We Want The Beatles, We Want The Beatles,* but I knew they were not going to oblige. They were, at that very moment, on their way to back to the Gresham Hotel in the back of an *Evening Herald* delivery van. We sat in our seats for a while, slightly mesmerised at what we had witnessed, until the mayhem abated and the confusion died down. Then I said to Anthony, "Well, what did you think of Beatlemania?"

"Beatlemania was great, but I don't know about The Beatles. I couldn't hear a word they were singing."

"Buy their records if you want to hear them," I said.

As we made our way out of the cinema the commotion was still going on in the street outside. We stood inside the glass doors of the cinema for a while and watched as the Gardai tried to disperse the crowds, which were refusing to leave the front of the Adelphi, hoping to get a glimpse of the fab four.

After about ten minutes or so, when much of the crowds had decided that they had enough and began to leave to catch their buses home, we came out of the Adelphi and decided to go for a cup of coffee where we would give our verdict on the gig.

As we made our way up Abbey Street towards O'Connell Street, though, I thought I heard someone call my name. I looked in the direction from which the sound came and on the opposite side of the street, waving over at me was Annette. She was with a fellow who looked a few years older than her. He was tall and heavyset with longish, dark hair, and he was wearing a long black coat which went well below his knees. His hands were in his pockets and he had a student-type coloured scarf around his neck in a manner that would later be termed "cool".

Annette was on his inside, linking him with her left arm in which hand she was also carrying a large black bag. She waved to me with her other hand.

She was wearing the beige woollen coat I remembered her wearing before and had a pink silk scarf on her head with her hair was loose underneath and falling onto her shoulders. She looked all grown up since I saw her last, very much as she looked when I first met her and at first I thought I was seeing things.

I excused myself to Rita and the others and said for them to go ahead and I would see them in a few minutes in the Palm Grove Cafe, then with my heart pounding I ran across to Annette.

"Were you at The Beatles?" Annette asked me excitedly as we stood looking at each other, with her companion standing silently, watching. I was in a state of utter confusion at this development. It was something else that had not happened the last time, but when the shock and surprise at seeing Annette began to wear off I eventually replied, "Yes, were you?"

"Yes, I was," she smiled. Then as an afterthought added, "Oh this is Edward, Edward Blake."

I was, by this point, in full control of my wits again, and so held my hand out to the guy who did not take his hands out of his pockets or make any move to respond to my gesture.

"Nice to meet you at last Eddie," I said. "I've heard a lot about you," and shrugged my shoulders at his sullen attitude before withdrawing my hand.

In the last timeframe Annette had told me of a guy she used to go out with for a while before she met me, Eddie Blake was his name so I reckoned that this must be him. She had said she did not like the way he kissed.

"How does he know me?" Eddie asked Annette, a bit peevishly I thought. Before Annette could think of a reply I interjected and said, "Don't worry about it Eddie, I know lots of things."

Eddie then turned to Annette and asked, "And how do you know him?" I was so delighted to see Annette again, but not with another guy on her arm, so I deliberately fanned the flames that were beginning to appear out of Eddie's nostrils.

"Oh Annette and I go back a long, long way Eddie. I'm surprised she has not mentioned me. She's told me a lot about you." I gave Annette a wink and a big grin.

"Andy, please not now," she said, unimpressed.

This familiarity between us only made Eddie more annoyed and he disengaged Annette's arm and said to her, "You go back a long way do you? Well you can go even longer, all the way to Ballyfermot. Goodbye Annette."

And with that Eddie Blake turned on his heel and walked out of her life.

Annette was furious with me. "What did you do that for?" she demanded. "You have no right to interfere in my life like that. Edward is a good friend of mine and you have given him a false impression of me and my relationship with you."

"It's all for the best," I said. "You know quite well it would never have worked out between you and him. You don't like the way he kisses."

Suddenly I took her in my arms and kissed her full on the

153

lips.

"Them's the kind of kisses you like," I said as she looked at me in shock.

"Would you like to go for a cup of coffee?" I asked while she was still trying to gather her wits, and I took her hand and led her across the road.

"My friends are in the Palm Grove."

"How did you know that?" she asked as she walked beside me, still confused.

"Because I've just told them I'd meet them there."

"Not that, how did you know I didn't like the way Edward kissed?"

"Annette, love, you told me the last time round." I smiled, and before she knew it we were walking into the Palm Grove cafe, hand in hand.

I pulled a chair over to the table and sat Annette down on it as the other five people looked on inquisitively.

"Hi everyone," I said. "Sorry about that little interruption but I've just been getting reacquainted with an old friend I lost contact with in the past and I didn't want it to happen again. This is Annette, Annette Kennedy, we've known each other for a long time now."

I then introduced Annette to each of them by mentioning their names and ordered our coffees. Anthony who had been observing Annette closely then asked, "Have I met you before?"

Before she could answer though, I said, "Full marks kid, you don't forget a pretty face do you? As a matter of fact you have, in a way, it was you who told me about Annette."

Anthony looked puzzled and said, "I did?"

"Remember the "fine thing" who served you highballs in a cafe in Newbridge a few years ago?" I said, and smiled at Annette.

"Is that you?" exclaimed Anthony, "I should have kept that information to myself!"

"Too late now," I laughed.

"How did you meet her, you never went to Newbridge?" Anthony then asked me.

"Oh, we met a long time ago, a very long time ago," I replied and squeezed Annette's hand.

I was conscious that we were excluding everyone else from the conversation so I changed the subject and asked how everyone enjoyed the show. There was fairly unanimous agreement that the Beatles were here to stay, especially if people ever got the chance to actually hear them, which had not been the case that night.

After a while Damien and Patricia said they had to go as they wanted to catch the last bus to Finglas. Patricia did not appear to be enjoying herself anyway so we bid them goodnight. Annette then attempted to rise from her chair saying she had to go as well or she would miss her bus, but I told her to stay where she was, that I was driving now and I'd drop her home.

She looked at me in surprise and said, "You've been busy since I last saw you, haven't you?"

"Just preparing for the day you'd walk back into my life again," I said, and smiled at her.

When Damien and Patricia left Annette, Anthony, Rita and I resumed the conversation.

Helen had been fairly quiet all night and despite efforts to involve her she was just not interested in joining in. I tried to involve her by asking her a few questions about the show, which she answered in monosyllables, and when I asked if she liked the kind of music The Beatles played, all she could come up with was, "It's alright I suppose."

She just, it appeared to me, did not want to be there and

after a short while, when we left her alone with her thoughts, she began to put her coat on and announced that she was going home.

It was late now and I knew that all the buses would be gone so I said that I would get my car and drive everyone home, but Helen did not want to wait while I went to the flats for the vehicle and when Anthony passed some comment about her impatience to get home she laid into him about his rudeness and the fact that she believed that he had ignored her all night. An exchange of words developed between them, much to our embarrassment, and Helen told Anthony that she would go home herself and for him not to bother contacting her again as it was "obvious that his interests were elsewhere." As she said this she was looking at Rita.

There was an embarrassed silence as Helen made her way out of the cafe, which was almost empty and about to close. Anthony said that it would be better if we all went to the flats rather than waiting in the cafe, so that's what we did. Walking up a deserted O'Connell Street in two pairs, Annette and Me and Anthony and Rita. On the way to the flats I took the opportunity to tell Annette how glad I was to see her again and how much I had missed her.

"You had Rita's shoulder to cry on so you could not have missed me that much," she replied with a touch of sarcasm, and, I thought, a hint of jealousy, which I was happy to see.

"There's nothing between Rita and me, she's just a friend I asked to the show, she ends up with Anthony," I told her and indicated to the two of them walking ahead and holding hands, oblivious to us.

Annette then smiled at me and gave me a kiss on the cheek before saying, "I missed you too," and held tight to my hand.

"You had Eddie to kiss away your blues," I smiled.

She just smiled back at me and said, "That other me had one big mouth, hadn't she?"

I kissed her gently on the lips and said, "I loved that big mouth – I still do."

After walking for a while in silence I then said, "So what's our future to be now? Where do we go from here? I told you I would respect your decision and I have done so."

"Yes, you did."

"It was not easy. In fact, I was almost outside your door one day, but decided to keep my word to you."

"Did you know you would see me tonight?" she then asked.

I stopped walking then and looked her straight in the eyes. "Annette, love, I had no idea I would see you tonight. Last time around you did not go to the concert. You told me that. I went with Anthony and Damien, we were on our own. Rita, Helen and Patricia were not with us the last time. I don't think we even knew them then. I had absolutely no reason to think I would see you tonight, and remember it was you who saw me and called over to me. I did not see you and if you had not called to me I would not have seen you. We would not have met like this. What's happening now is all new to me too, this did not happen the last time."

Anthony and Rita were deep in conversation ahead of us and I said to Annette, pointing to them, "This is not at all the way things happened before, not for any of us. I'm driving now, I never did that the last time, it was you who drove when we did get a car. This whole thing is turning into a magical mystery tour for me. It seems I did something to change the future by contacting you ahead of the time we were due to meet."

"Andy," she said "I really like you, I like your company and..."

"My kisses?" I quickly interjected, smiling.

"Yes, those too," she smiled back. "If we were only meeting now for the first time I would be prepared to let the relationship develop naturally, but it's hard for me to be with someone who knows everything that is going to happen to us… to me. I feel I have no control over the choices that will be made if you know everything that is going to happen. I'd never know for certain just how much you might be manipulating situations to bring about the result you want. You did it when I met your mother, and you did it again tonight, using what you knew about Edward and me to get rid of him and get what you wanted."

We let Anthony and Rita walk ahead and stood on the corner of Parnell Street facing the Rotunda Hospital as I said to Annette, "That's all changed now, I don't know everything that's going to happen to us. I did not know that I would meet you tonight. Our lives seem to have been changed precisely because I meddled in it. It can never be the way it was the last time now. I did not know you at this time in the '65 timeframe. You did not go to The Beatles concert with Eddie Blake the last time… and by the way you called him Eddie the last time, why the formality this time calling him Edward?"

She just looked at me and shrugged her shoulders, "I don't know."

"See, everything is different from what I remember. This is all new to both of us. I have no idea what's going to happen to us from here on in, as a matter of fact you have more knowledge of that than I have as it is you who will decide if our relationship… well, you hold all the aces now Annette. I told you that I would respect your decision and not try to contact you and I have done so, yet still we have managed to meet. Maybe destiny has intervened to set us back on the path we should be on, but irrespective of that I will still respect your decision. It's still all up to you where we go from here. Only you can decide what happens to us from now on."

Annette remained silent as we stood on the footpath and watched Anthony and Rita turn down the lane towards the back of the flats and the car.

"But you still know so many things about me. You knew about Edward... Eddie, and you used that knowledge to get rid of him tonight. How can I be sure you won't do things like that again if something happens that you do not like and want to change in the future?"

"You were never going to stay with Eddie Blake," I responded. "And you know that."

"But if I wasn't I want that to be my decision not yours. I don't want you interfering in my life to hasten changes you know are coming, can't you see that?"

She was right, I had breached her boundaries by what I had done, and in doing so I had made her distrustful of me and made it less likely that she would ever consent to being my wife. Although she and Eddie were never going to go far romantically, I should not have interfered in the matter. I remained silent as I simply did not know what to say to get anywhere near restoring the trust I feared I had lost.

We resumed walking across the road and as we turned into Granby Lane Annette asked, "Well? What have you got to say? That's twice you've interfered in my life, twice that is that I know of."

"I swear to you they were the only times I did so. I give you my word here and now that I will never do so again, no matter what the situation is. I will let events take their own course. You have my solemn word on that."

"I'd like to believe you, but the process by which things

come about tell me more about what you are than what you say," she replied with a wry smile on her face.

I could only smile when I heard her speak those words and replied, "Do you know what Annette? If you put music to those words you'd have a song."

When we reached the car in Granby Lane Anthony and Rita were leaning against the side of it, Anthony with his arm around Rita's shoulder.

"Do you mind if I go as far as Phibsborough with Rita and then you can drop me off on your way back to Ballyfermot?" Anthony asked as we, all four, quite willingly and wordlessly acknowledged the seamless re-coupling that had occurred.

"No, that's OK," I said and smiled at Annette as Anthony and Rita sat in the back seat and Rita lay her head on his shoulder.

Annette sat beside me in the front and we set off to leave the girl who had started the night as my date home, with her new boyfriend, who in a few years time would be her husband. How strange are the ways of time travelling?

The roads were almost empty of traffic and we got to Rita's house in a matter of minutes. Anthony and Rita got out when I stopped at the corner, and while I turned the car back in the direction of the city he left her to her to her gate.

Annette and I remained sitting in the car while they stood at the gate, seemingly reluctant to part, and then Anthony kissed Rita on the lips and said something to her to, which she nodded her head at. Then he walked back to the car looking very pleased with himself. Little was said on the way back to town and I let Anthony off at the Parnell Monument as we continued down a very quiet and empty O'Connell Street.

As we approached the junction of Abbey Street I stopped

the car and pointed out some of the damage that had been caused to shops and cars earlier in the night, due to the aftermath of the Beatles concert.

Was it like this before? Annette wanted to know and I told her it was the very same. I also told her to be sure to get a copy of the *Evening Press* the next day, as it would have a great picture of a Garda picking a youth up by the arse of his trousers and the scruff of the neck and throwing him out of the crowd.

As we drove to Ballyfermot we engaged in small talk about how her father was getting on in his still relatively new job and about the increase in her family. We also spoke about the show and Annette said how much she liked The Beatles music, saying it was great to dance to, which I knew, having danced to their music many a time with her in the last timeframe. She then asked if their popularity would last, but I did not want to go into specifics and was not forthcoming with that information, saying only that she would just have to wait and see as the future as I knew it seemed to have changed.

I was trying to forget all about my past life and concentrating now on winning over the love of the Annette of this life. I was hoping I could persuade her to give me the chance to show her that we could start this new relationship on an equal basis and to do that I was determined to ditch my past once and for all. I stopped the car at the entrance to the short adjunct to Le Fanu Road, where Annette's house was situated, just before the old hump backed bridge, which led to the Naas Road but she made no move to get out of the car and I did not get out of the driver's seat to open the door for her.

"Do you want to see me again?" Annette asked as we both sat in silence.

"Of course I do. Do you want to see me?"

"I suppose I'll have to, now that you've frightened my other fella away," she smiled.

I reached over to pull her to me but she just gave me a tender kiss on the lips and said, "It's late, mammy will be wondering where I am, I better go on in."

I released my hold on her arm, sighed a big sigh of relief and said, "I'll pick you up about eight tomorrow night, OK?"

"Where will we go?"

"Who knows? The future is all ours to make of it what we will." I reached across her to open the door and she stepped out of the car.

I waited until she walked the short distance to her house and waved as she opened the gate and walked to the door. I was elated at the way the night had turned out. I had absolutely no idea when I picked Rita up earlier that she would be ending the night with her future husband and I would be back in with a chance of making Annette my wife.

There was something great and exciting about not knowing what the future had in store. It would not be like the last time, that was now certain, and in a way I was glad of that. It would now be like meeting Annette for the first time and falling in love all over again, and with all the excitement and anticipation that would bring.

Two lives were about to merge into one and neither of us knew where that would lead to. One thing I was determined to do this time, that I had not done as often as I should have in the past, was to appreciate the type of person Annette was and not to hurt her, inadvertently though it was, as I had done so many time before.

There was also the issue of her passing, which would have to be confronted at some time, but I still hoped, that if that time came again, I would be in a position to prolong her life.

Chapter seventeen

I SAW Annette every second night after that and things were going from good to great between us. She was now inclined to believe what I had told her and although I had said that I hoped we could do it all again, that decision still remained hers to make. I met her parents again and reminded them of our first meeting in Newbridge in 1960.

"Oh yes," Mary had exclaimed. "You brought down some songs for Willie Rogers. I believe he's singing with a ballad group now, they must have been good songs you gave him."

Everything was going so well now and the past was becoming less of an issue between us. It was the future that was occupying my mind now.

Then suddenly out of nowhere on, Sunday the 17th of November, the past caught up with me. I was to meet Annette that night and we had planned to go dancing. I was listening to the news on the radio at lunch time and the newscaster mentioned the fact that President Kennedy was to visit Dallas during the week, as part of the Presidential campaign of 1964. I had almost forgotten about it when suddenly I was brought back to the horror that I knew was about to unfold. Friday, November 22nd, 1963 in Dallas was here again and I became very uneasy. *Would it happen again in this timeframe or were things changed sufficiently to cause it not to happen? By my knowing about it, had I the power to prevent it happening if the same conditions prevailed this time? Should I even try to prevent it? If I did try would it all be in vain and would history repeat itself anyway?* I agonised all afternoon over what I should do or could do to prevent it happening again.

When I met Annette that night I was not much in the mood for dancing and asked her if she would mind if we did not go. At first she thought I had not got sufficient money and said that she would pay if that was the reason for not going. I assured her that was not the reason and said there was something on my mind that I wanted to talk to her about but that I'd prefer if we went somewhere quiet to talk about it.

I don't know what she thought it was, maybe that I was having second thoughts about our future together and had changed my mind about her, but for a moment she became very concerned and worried looking. I assured her that it had nothing to do with the way I felt about her and that I loved her and wanted to marry her if that's what she wanted – and that nothing would ever change that. After a few more probes about what was on my mind, which I parried by saying that it would be better if we waited and sat down and discussed it in full, I drove into town and parked the car in the parking space in the middle of O'Connell Street and we went to the small bar in Princes Street beside the Capitol. When we found a table for two in a quiet corner of the room I went to the bar and ordered a pint of Guinness and a glass of orange juice, which Annette had asked me to get her, despite me offering wine.

I brought the drinks to the table and sat beside Annette and I took a large mouthful of beer, almost half the glass, and put the glass back on the table. I did not know where to begin or how to tell her what was on my mind and began rambling all over the place about how hard I was trying to forget my past, but I was finding it very hard when from time to time something reminded me of something from it that I wanted to forget.

Eventually Annette got so confused with what I was trying to say that she just said she did not understand a word of it and if there was something bothering me I should just say what it was and not be wasting time with incoherent chatter.

"I really don't know how to say this," I said. "You know I've tried to put my past existence behind me and not bring it into our future, but earlier today a part of that past was thrust firmly back into my life – and this event will, before this week is out, shock the entire world. My problem is that I know about this terrible event, I know about it now almost a week before it is due to happen and if the same conditions prevail it's possible that I could prevent it happening. But if I do that I will be causing a huge, a monumental, change in the course of world history as I know it, and I have no idea where or what that would lead to."

Annette listened in silence to what I said and then asked, "Does this event involve you?"

Her question brought a little light relief to my mind and I laughed as I told her, "No, it certainly did not the last time but by my knowing of it, it could this time. That's why I wanted to talk to you about it. Maybe, just maybe, I could prevent it happening this time, but should I try and in doing so change the course of world history in the process?"

"What happened?" Annette then asked.

"Someone was murdered."

"Oh, you have to prevent that," she quickly replied. "You can't let someone be murdered if you have the power to prevent it."

"But it means I'd be meddling in the future and you said I should not do that," I reminded her.

She was silent for a moment as she pondered my answer and then she asked, "Who was murdered?"

"President Kennedy," I said.

"Oh my God," she gasped and put her hands to her mouth. "You can't let that happen."

"I don't know if I can prevent it," I replied. "What do I do? Tell people I've lived before and know what's going to happen next week? Who do I tell that would believe me? They would think I was mad and have me locked up. It's not that easy, and anyway I'm not 100% sure that it will happen this time. Look at me, my life is different from what it was, different from the way I remember it being the last time, so who's to know that other things may be changed as well?"

"When will it happen?"

"Next Friday, the 22nd of November, 1963." The mention of the day of infamy sent a shiver down my spine.

"Next Friday? This is Sunday, you don't have much time if you're going to do or say something."

"I know," I absently replied as terrible images of the assassination came into my mind's eye. "That's why I needed to talk to someone, to talk to you, about it. My whole mind is in turmoil and I have no idea what I should do." I could feel my eyes filling with tears.

"What happened, how was he murdered?"

"He was shot while he was travelling in a motorcade through Dallas, but it was all a bit of a mystery as to who actually shot him. Even as late as 2010 no one knew for certain who pulled the trigger, though the CIA, the Central Intelligence Agency, were thought to have been involved in it.

There was, what many believed, to be a massive cover up

instigated immediately after the assassination and many unexplained deaths of people connected to the events in Dallas that day began happening shortly after it. All done, it was thought, to suppress the true facts of that day ever becoming public knowledge. Because the CIA were widely believed to have been involved, it was believed by some to have effectively been a coup. A guy by the name of Lee Harvey Oswald was put forward as the prime suspect, but many thought he was set up by the CIA and only a patsy for the coup, if that's what it was. He, Oswald, was shot while in custody and never stood trial. He was actually shot in the Dallas police station on the Sunday after the Kennedy assassination, having been arrested by the Dallas police for the suspected murder of a police officer who was attempting to question him on the afternoon of the assassination."

"How was he shot in the police station?" Annette asked in surprise.

"A small time local mobster by the name of Jack Ruby, who was on friendly terms with the cops, and was possibly on the pay role of the CIA, had the run of the station and just went in on the Sunday when Oswald was being moved to another location. In the full glare of live television cameras and a station full of police officers and reporters he pulled a gun and shot Oswald in the stomach.

As I said there was all kinds of speculation and rumours as to who was actually involved in the assassination for years afterwards. Everyone from the CIA to Castro, the Mafia, the Ku Klux Klan, the Russians, Edgar Hoover and the FBI were all linked to it, and even combinations of them all.

Had "Bang Bang" lived in America I'm sure he would have been a suspect too. Conspiracy theories were ten a penny, but nobody, apart from the killer or killers, ever knew for certain who really was involved. It was one of the great unsolved mysteries of the age."

"What are you going to do?" Annette eventually asked, after digesting the history/future lesson.

"I honestly don't know," I told her. "What can I do? Walk into a Garda station and report a murder that has not yet happened? It's me who would be arrested and locked up."

"But if you don't do anything and it happens again…"

"And if I do and it doesn't as a result of my action, then I've changed history as it may have been meant to be and all the things that happened as a consequence of the Kennedy assassination will not happen this time… and many things will happen that maybe were not meant to happen as a result of him living and continuing to be the president of the USA…"

"Like what? What's more important, a man not being murdered or how history may turn out?" Annette demanded.

"The presidential succession in America for one thing. Men that I remember being president may not become president this time, the war in Vietnam for another, relations with Russia and Cuba. These are just a few of the things that will be affected if Kennedy is not assassinated next Friday. If he lives I'm very sure Vietnam will have a different outcome from what I remember, because from what I read subsequently, Kennedy, had he not been assassinated had plans to pull American troops out of there and while that may have been a good thing for America it could well have involved many more deaths elsewhere in Southeast Asia. Then there are personal family matters to be considered, the lives of very many of his family were affected by the assassination and certain things happened as a direct result of him being killed, things that will not happen if the assassination is prevented."

Annette pondered what I said and reached over and held

my hand before saying, "Only you can decide what to do, I can't tell you."

It was not what I was hoping to hear and it was no great help to me in the dilemma I faced. I had this terrible knowledge about an event that would change the world, and maybe, just maybe I could prevent it happening, but if I did then would the world be a better place as a result of my action or would it be changed in the worst way?

I knew pretty much how things panned out after the assassination and although the world went through a rough time with the upsurge of violence in the Middle East and the rise of terrorism, as well as the subsequent wars in Iraq and Afghanistan, if Kennedy lived would things be any different?

Indeed would things be worse? Would they succeed in finding out who really planned the assassination, and if Castro or the Russians were behind it would the American people demand retribution and want to exact revenge from them for their act of aggression in trying to kill an American president on American soil? And possibly bring about a high octane situation between America and Russia, like the Cuban stand off, only this time would anyone back down? These were my concerns as I tried to decide what course of action I should take.

Then there was my own personal situation to consider. If I spoke out and I was proved right, whether or not any action was taken on my warning or whether I was taken seriously before the assassination, if Kennedy was killed as I predicted he would be, I would become the focus of worldwide attention after the event. It would be impossible for me to lead any kind of a normal life and the very thing I had wished for, the chance to live my life again with Annette, would be an impossibility.

There would be the added danger that the major world powers, like America and Russia might think it a good idea to have in their custody someone who had lived before and knew what was around the corner, so to speak.

I brought all these things up with Annette and after about three hours, four pints and a few glasses of white wine later, because Annette felt she needed something stronger than orange juice after hearing what I had told her, the barman began to call time on our discussion about the future. We reluctantly decided that the best course of action was to let events take their own course, and hoped, beyond hope, that just maybe it would not happen this time. That the, to me, infamous names of Oswald, Ruby and The Texas School Book Depositary in Dealey Plaza, Dallas, would not become part of world folklore again.

We met every night that week and although we had decided not to do anything or say anything about the assassination we continued to talk about the possible consequences of the decision we had made. I bought a newspaper every day and followed all the news bulletins on radio and television in the hope that I would hear that the president's trip to Dallas had been cancelled, but nothing was reported along those lines.

I had never before discussed or told Annette, apart from the details of our own life, anything important about future world events up to then. The Kennedy assassination was the first and only thing I had ever spoken about in this way. But because I had spoken about the Kennedys, and alluded to their life after the assassination, Annette, like most women would have, wanted to know what happened to Jackie after JFK's death, and I felt obliged after what I had confided in her already to tell her all I could remember about Jackie's life after the presidential years, including her marriage to

Aristotle Onassis.

By the time Friday came around Annette was better informed about that Kennedy family than she was about her own.

The last time JFK was assassinated I remembered well that I was at home in Dominick Street getting ready to meet my friends to go to the pictures. I did not, of course, know Annette then, but this time if it was going to happen all over again I was going to be with her when Charles Mitchell interrupted *My Three Sons* on Telefís Eireann to announce to the nation that President Kennedy had been shot.

After coming home from work (I was at that time working in a factory that assembled television aerials) I had some fish and chips for my tea and washed before going straight out to Ballyfermot where I surprised Mary and Bill by my early appearance. Annette I could see was a bit tense and not her usual happy self and after a short cuddle in the hall we sat on the sofa in front of the fire with our eyes firmly fixed on the television screen. I silently prayed that the programme would finish without interruption. Shortly after 6.30pm though, the black and white pictures suddenly flickered and the screen turned into a snowlike haze for a second or two and then, looking straight at us, was the unsmiling and serious face of Charles Mitchell. My heart sank.

The first reports were sketchy and only said that shots had been fired at the presidential motorcade as it was passing through the centre of Dallas. It was thought that the president had been hit but it was not known if his injuries were serious or not. The motorcade had sped to a hospital. There would be further bulletins later if there was anything more to report. Mitchell concluded his report and the station went back to its normal programming.

Bill and Mary were in the kitchen with the younger

children having their tea when the first bulletin came on and after it I told Annette to tell them to come out and look at the television so that they would see history in the making.

My Three Sons ended and a sports programme, hosted by Brendan O'Reilly, commenced – but it had no sooner started than Brendan could be seen looking uneasily to his left and right before announcing that they were breaking to go to the newsroom for an announcement.

The screen went black and immediately the picture came back with the solemn and visibly shaken face of Charles Mitchell. In an emotional state and with a choked voice he told the nation that president Kennedy was dead. While Mary and Bill and the rest of the family gathered around the television in a state of shock and silence, I took Annette's hand and, unnoticed, we went outside.

The last time while I was shocked by the assassination I do not remember crying, but outside as we sat on the steps in the cold November air, and I held Annette close to me, we both cried bitter tears.

"I could have prevented it," I sobbed. "I could have done something."

"It was meant to be," Annette cried while trying to console me. "You could not have done anything, it was meant to be."

We sat for a while on the steps until the cold began to make our teeth chatter. We then composed ourselves and went back into the warmth of the house to sit with Mary and Bill as the night's events unfolded all over again.

Once more Officer Tippit was shot and shortly after a suspect was arrested in a cinema in the Oak Cliff area of Dallas. Lee Harvey Oswald, a name so familiar to me, was once again introduced into the vocabulary of a world in a state of paralysis. As the confused details of the assassination, which I knew would still be confused almost fifty years later, were relayed, all I could do was watch as history repeated itself. I left the house at about 10.30pm and drove home, my mind in turmoil. It was too late for regret though, all I could do was watch the horror of the aftermath unfold again.

I woke early on Saturday morning, but in truth I had been awake almost all night going over and over in my mind what I could have done or should have done, but it was all a futile exercise now. Kennedy was dead and I had done nothing.

Like the last time the rooftops of the city were glistening white, covered under a heavy frost and after a cup of tea and a brief discussion with my father, mother and brother about the assassination I went out and bought a paper.

At lunchtime I met Annette at the gate of O'Dea's and we went to a small cafe in Liffey Street for lunch. Annette told me that not much work had been done in the factory that morning, even though they were in on overtime, as everyone was talking about the assassination and no one could concentrate on work.

"I hope you didn't say anything about what you know," I said.

"Of course I didn't, what do you take me for?" she replied, highly annoyed that I should have even asked the question.

"It's not over yet, Ruby has still to come into the picture, and I mean that quite literally," I said.

"Oh God, poor Oswald has still to be killed. Can you not do something, anything?" she implored.

"I can't, not now. The chain of events has started and nothing can be done at this stage to stop it happening. It will be just like before."

I said this as much to convince myself as Annette. If I was going to do anything I should have done it before the assassination, it was too late now I had to, like everyone else, watch the carnage unfold.

Kennedy and Tippit were dead and the next day Oswald would join them in the unresolved story of November 22nd, 1963.

I did not have the stomach to watch Ruby shoot Oswald again so on Sunday afternoon I met Annette in town and we went to the Adelphi Cinema to see *King of Kings*, a biblical epic. When we came out onto the street in the late evening the town was abuzz with people standing in small groups discussing the latest murder in Dallas.

After the weekend of killings, we did not speak of the assassination again. I knew it had a traumatic effect on Annette and brought the knowledge that I also knew when she would die crashing back into her mind. I tried to get things back to where they were between us before all the disruption of the weekend, to the night of The Beatles concert when I felt Annette was prepared to give our relationship the chance to start afresh. I knew now beyond all doubt that she believed me, so it was up to me now to try to get her to fall in love with me all over again – and that had to be my focus.

I also had to convince her that although the Kennedy assassination had happened as I had predicted it would, not everything in the future needed to be the same, particularly her passing.

I had chosen not to do anything about the assassination for fear that interfering in such a momentous event would change world history, but I was prepared – more than prepared, I was determined – if the conditions were the same to interfere and save her life this time.

Chapter eighteen

IN the last timeframe I had asked Annette to marry me at Christmas, 1966 and she had said yes and we got engaged at Easter 1967. As Christmas 1963 approached I decided I would push my luck, and relying on her state of mind being receptive towards me because of the recent events, and I asked her to marry me.

I think I was more nervous this time than I had been in 1966. I knew that if she said no this time, after all that had happened, she probably would not change her mind and that would be the end of our relationship because I had no intention of hanging around and being a nuisance to her if she was not going to marry me.

With that thought in mind I had to be very careful how I approached proposing to her.

The last time Annette insisted that I ask Bill for her hand before we got engaged, and after a long period of hesitation on my part I did so – but I had no intention of going down that road again. Not out of any disrespect to Bill, but I truly believed that Annette was my wife and I had done all the formalities the last time around, so I was determined that if she said yes and wanted me to go through all that again I would have to find an excuse good enough to sideline the issue.

One way out of the dilemma, I thought, was to make it an

non issue by just getting engaged without saying anything to anyone until it was all over, and in that way there would be no need for all the formal requests for her hand. I hatched a plan that I hoped would be romantic enough to sweep Annette off her feet and leave her with no option but to say yes.

The Shangri-La Restaurant on Dalkey Harbour had been a favourite of ours the last time, but so far this time we had not been to it – in fact I was not sure if it was in existence yet in this timeframe. I checked the phonebook and was happy to see that it was. I took a calculated risk and booked a table for two on Saturday night, the 21st of December, without telling Annette. I picked her up at 7pm, much earlier than I normally would have done, having told her to wear a dress she could dance in, but not where we were going.

She was very curious but I said that it was a surprise and all would be revealed when we got there.

The dress she choose to wear that night was one I remembered her wearing in our last life, one that I thought she looked fabulous in. It had red and white polka dots, cut low at the neck with a tight waist and a flowing knee-length skirt. She looked fantastic in it and I could not wait to hold her tight as we danced. When I went into the house to get her and saw her in the outfit I was rendered speechless and almost cried with joy at seeing my past come alive again.

In the presence of Mary and Bill and her younger sisters I couldn't help it and took her in my arms and kissed her passionately, which I think embarrassed her a bit but I did not care, she was my wife after all.

Mary, seeing my reaction to Annette half jokingly but wholly in earnest said, "Make sure you bring her back in one piece, we don't want a Spring wedding this year."

"I wouldn't spring that on you. Would Winter suit you

better?" I laughed and took Annette's hand as she picked her coat up off the chair and I led her to the car.

"Where are we going?" she asked, as soon as we were in the car. Before I answered I again took her in my arms and kissed her on the lips.

"I always loved you wearing that dress, it makes you look so sexy and because you're looking so fabulous I'm taking you to Shangri-La."

"Where's that?" she asked as she settled herself in the seat and threw her coat into the back.

"You'll see," I said and headed for town and the Dun Laoghaire Road.

On the way, because Annette looked so beautiful she was distracting me and I wanted to hold her and tell her how much I loved her, I stopped at the seafront in Dun Laoghaire and parked the car facing towards the dark cold sea. Then, under the winter star-filled sky we spent about twenty minutes kissing and cuddling until my passion had abated, and we decided to move on. We were then running late and I didn't want to risk a less favourable position than the one I had asked for.

It was just as I remembered it. A small, dimly lit room with a raised platform that was used as a stage and small square tables covered in red and white check tablecloths, with a lighted candle in an old wine bottle on each. The three piece combo were playing *Night and Day* and in doing so, was creating a perfectly romantic atmosphere.

We were shown to our table by a waitress and the whole scene, I felt, was like something straight out of an old black and white film and I think Annette half expected Humphrey Bogart to be sitting at the next table with Lauren Bacall.

When we sat down she, looking around her, took in the whole scene obviously enchanted, and asked me,

"How did you know about this place?"

"We used to come here in our last life," I told her.

"You're last life. I've never been here before," she reminded me.

"You were, but you don't remember," I laughed.

The waitress, a middle-aged lady, who had shown us to the table then came back and gave us a menu and as she did she commented to Annette on her dress, telling her how nice it was.

I laughed and said, "That, sure that's just an old thing she's had for ages," and winked at Annette.

We ordered our meal and a bottle of red house wine and sat back listening to the music. I raised my glass to Annette and said, "To our future, may it be as happy for both of us as the last one was for me – and may it last longer."

Annette said nothing but raised her glass and took a sip from it. The combo was now playing *As Time Goes By* so while we were waiting for the food to arrive I asked Annette to dance. She was, at first, reluctant to do so as there was nobody else on the floor, but I stood up, took her hand and led her onto the floor in front of the little raised platform where I held her tight and we danced until long after our meal had been placed on our table.

When eventually we decided to step off the dancefloor and sit down we were surprised and embarrassed to get a round of applause from the other diners, whom we had been oblivious to. When we sat down the waitress came and took our meals away as they were almost cold and said she would bring fresh food for us. I was delighted that Annette seemed to be enjoying the night so much and when we finished our meals we got up and danced again, though this time we did not have the floor to ourselves.

As the night was coming to an end we sat and finished the

wine and took in our surroundings.

"This is a lovely place, we must come here again," Annette said.

"We will and we did," I replied. "It was one of our favourite places the last time.

"The last time I don't remember," Annette reminded me. "I know, but you enjoyed it every bit as much as you did tonight, and you will enjoy it again, I promise you." I told her and kissed her.

Annette remained silent and I then gambled with my future.

"Annette, love," I began. "I know you don't remember all the things I do, all the things I've told you about our previous life together, but I want you to believe me when I say we were really happy. We had a good life and I want the chance for us to live that life again. That's the reason I brought you here tonight. The Shangri–La was important to us the last time, it's where we became engaged and I wanted to see if it still had the magic it had for us before. Judging by how much I think you enjoyed yourself, I'm guessing it still has."

Then I held her hand and as she looked into my eyes I said, "Annette Marie Kennedy, will you marry me?"

For what seemed like an eternity she said nothing, then just as I thought I had blown it and was anticipating a no, a big broad smile spread across her face and she took my face in her hands, kissed me on the lips and said, "How could any girl say no to a proposal like that? Of course I'll marry you... again."

All I could do, at hearing her accept my proposal, was close my eyes and raise my head to the ceiling as I cried, "Thank you, thank you, thank you," to whoever it was that had given me this chance.

The chance to live my life all over again, with Annette.

Chapter nineteen

BEFORE proposing to Annette I had told my mother and father that I was seeing her again, though I had not brought her up to the flat. They were both delighted with the news, particularly my mother, who commented when I told her, that she always knew we would get back together and that it was always "only a matter of time."

Over the past few months she had often asked me about Annette and when I said that the relationship was over had invariably said something like, "Ah well sure maybe the time is not right just yet" or "there's a time for everything," and smiled a wry smile, which I always thought was a little strange.

Delighted at the news she urged me to bring Annette up to the flat straight away and so, with Annette having agreed to marry me, as she had put it herself, "again," I did just that and wasted no time in reintroducing her to my family and ma's ham sandwiches again.

Mary and Bill, like my own parents, were delighted when we told them we intended to get married. I did not, this time, have to go through the ordeal of asking Bill for Annette's hand. Like the last time, however, we arranged a social meeting between our parents and just like before they bonded very well. My father and Mary discovered, once again, that they had been near neighbours in Queen

Street many years before, so all seemed to be well on that front.

We set the date of our wedding for Sunday, the 1st of August, 1965 – the day we met the first time around. Apart from that little bit of Deja vu I was determined that I would not guide or manipulate the wedding in the same direction as it had gone in 1968. I did not want Annette to feel she was being led down the same wedding path I knew so well.

I had told her all about our last wedding so I let her decide what the plans and arrangements would be this time, after all this was her first wedding. I wanted her to have the wedding she wanted this time, not the one I remembered. So I took a step back from all the planning and let her decide how our wedding day would be. While the church venue would be the same I knew Annette wanted the honeymoon destination and the hotel to be different. I had no problem with that, I was just happy that she had fallen in love with me again and let her get on with planning everything the way she wanted it.

The last time around we did not have very much money so we had to start our married life in a small artisan dwelling on the North Strand. This time I cheated and with the knowledge I had about the times we were living in won enough money on bets, particularly Shelbourne's defeat of Portuguese side Belinennese in the Fairs Cup competition and Team Spirit's win at 18 to 1 in that year's Grand National, to be able to put a deposit on a new house in the Walkinstown/ Green Hills area, which was being developed at that time. I remembered in the previous timeframe we had looked at houses in this area and Annette really liked them, but they were out of our reach financially. This time I was in the position to be able to tell her to pick the house she wanted in an estate halfway between the city and the mountains.

Because things were going so well between us, and I was trying so hard to banish all thought of my previous existence, and acting as if this was the first time we were to be married, it was only after putting the deposit on the house Annette had chosen that I noticed that it was directly in line with and under the Hell Fire Club – the very mountain Annette, in our previous life, was buried on. Every time I'd open the door in that house I'd be confronted with the past, and the future, and the pain of my last life. After noticing this and without saying why, I tried to change her mind about buying the house, even suggesting that we could go a bit higher in price and buy a house near the sea, but to no avail – she had set her heart on that one.

I did not want to arouse any suspicions in her mind about my attempts to get her to change her mind so I did not pursue it too vigorously, consoling myself with the knowledge that we would not be moving in until after the wedding in August '65 and something might happen to change her mind between now and then.

Before the end of 1964 the hotel and honeymoon destination were decided on. The reception, for 70 guests – 20 more than the last time – would be in The Royal Marine Hotel in Dun Laoghaire, which had a sea view that we both loved, and was also near enough to where the reception was held the last time. The honeymoon was planned for Torremolinos on the Costa del Sol. When all these details were settled we began to relax and look forward to August 1965. Having a bit more money this time round certainly made things a lot easier and apart from my little raids on the bookies from time to time, I was also working in a relatively well-paid job in a domestic appliance company while Annette was still in O'Dea's, so there was none of the worry and stress I remembered from the last time about the planning difficulties with the house in the North Strand.

We were both drinking a lot younger this time, and a lot more, than we had the last time, and from time to time after a few drinks Annette would sometimes ask me to tell her about our life the last time. I knew that she really wanted to know about her death, but I did not want to go there and always tried to steer the conversation away from that subject by reminding her that this was a new life for us both. We were doing things now that we had never done in the past and I wanted to get on with this life and forget all about my last one.

I was worried about these developments though, our drinking and Annette's curiosity, and it was making me uneasy. Drink was never a problem with us the last time and I did not want it to become a part of our way of life this time as I knew where it could lead to. I also knew that if Annette was asking these questions when she had drink taken the same questions must have been on her mind when she was sober, and this worried me also. I realised more and more that I should never have told her that she had passed away in our previous life as knowledge like that was bound to unnerve anyone, especially a young girl, which I often forgot Annette was.

But however much I regretted my mistake there was no way I could undo that damage now so I decided that all I could do was insist that I did not want to discuss Annette's passing when either, or both of us, had drink on us. But living in the shadow of Annette's burial place would be a daily reminder to me of our other life and what was possibly ahead of me again and the sadness and pain I endured when it ended. I would never be able to raise my eyes to that mountain without being reminded that in another life

Annette was buried there.

I thought long and hard about this problem and how I would handle it if it happened. She knew she had passed away and I knew it was on her mind, it had to be, so I started thinking that maybe it would be better if, instead of her asking me about it, I should be the one who broached the subject and handled the situation in my own way, in my own time – but not yet, the wedding was approaching fast and I did not want anything to spoil the happiness I knew we would both derive from becoming husband and wife again.

I was now more than three years back in this timeframe and I had witnessed JFK's election as president of America, his visit to Ireland and his assassination all over again, as well as seeing The Beatles dominate the world of popular music once more. The Theatre Royal had closed and been pulled down again and we had danced to *The Hucklebuck* and *The Twist* and *Ran All The Way Home to The Candy Store On The Corner* as I watched the Showbands sweep across the land all over again. Yuri Gagarin, once more, became the first man to walk in space on the 12th of April, 1961, and the first public live transatlantic television transmission, which spawned the hit tune *Telstar* was relayed to an amazed world in glorious black and white on July 23rd 1962. RTE, or Telsfis Eireann as it was then known, was launched from the Gresham Hotel to a snow-covered nation on the 31st of December, 1961 and on the 6th of June, 1962 The Late Late Show began its record-breaking run, which was still going strong when I rolled down the hill in the Phoenix Park in 2010. The Berlin Wall was built again, Marilyn Monroe and Pope John the twenty third died again and Martin Luther King had a dream in Washington, on the 28th of August, 1963.

All these events occurred exactly as I remembered them from my previous life, even though I was leading a completely different one by comparison. It seemed a paradoxical situation. How could I be living a different life in seemingly the same circumstances and through events that had already happened? Apart from the Kennedy assassination I never told Annette about these things before they happened, though after some of them made the headlines she did ask about them and if I had known they would happen. I never denied knowing about them, but always tried to play it down by saying I forgot as I was now fully involved living in this time and was not dwelling on what had gone before.

And that was the truth, I really was fully committed to living this life as if it was my first, and Annette and I, or at least I, were doing it all for the first time.

The love between us was just as strong, if not stronger now than it had been in that last life because I was now more conscious of, and more sensitive to, Annette's needs and I followed her lead. I also wanted to believe that by changing our lifestyle this time we could somehow cause the outcome to be different and it need not necessarily end in the same way or the same time as before.

By the end of 1964 there was nothing to do but wait for August to come around, a huge contrast to the last time. Because I was now driving we spent a lot of time going to places I remembered we went to the last time, though I very often did not tell Annette the reason for our trips there as I did not want her to think that I was trying to recreate the previous life. I personally found it a great experience to see the changes in the various locations, to the way I last remembered them in 2010.

There was one place we went to that Christmas that we

had not been to in the last lifetime, though we had heard of it. Doyle's dance hall was a corrugated shed located on the junction of the Tallaght Road, just before the right hand turn onto the Blessington Road.

When we moved to Tallaght in 1973 its dance hall days were over and it was a billiard hall. But we had heard so many stories about its golden era that I decided I would take the opportunity to see what all the fuss was about. I picked Annette up on St Stephen's night, not telling her where we were going, only that we were going to a dance. It was a Saturday and we drove out to Tallaght up the steep dark Greenhills Road, stopping for a few moments to look at our new home, which was at that time in the course of construction.

The night was clear and I glanced up at the mountains in the background, and prominent on the summit was the dark hulking shape of The Hellfire Club, which seemed to dominate the skyline and sent a shiver down my spine. I quickly ushered Annette back into the car and we left the site. When we came to the entrance of the estate and I turned left rather than to the right, which would have brought us back in the direction of town, Annette wanted to know where we were going.

"We're going to Tallaght," I told her.

"Tallaght? There's no dance hall in Tallaght."

"There is. Doyle's shed."

"I never heard of that."

By this time we were approaching the junction at Tallaght village with the Priory on our right hand side. As I turned the corner I said to Annette, "Straight ahead is Doyle's Emporium, careful the light's don't blind you."

"Where is it? I don't see anything," she said straining her eyes.

Unlike the time I remembered when we lived in Tallaght there was no problem parking anywhere we liked and so I parked the car on the large kerb outside Kennedy's hardware shop, just up a bit from Doyle's, and I helped Annette out of the car.

From across the road we could hear the sound of singing from the Porterhouse/Dragon Inn and further down the road it was total darkness apart from the weak lights from Molloy's.

"Where are we?" Annette wanted to know as we walked the short distance to the door of the corrugated shed.

"I told you, Doyle's dance hall in Tallaght," I said as I gave the lady on the door three shillings to gain entry.

Another door was then opened for us by an elderly man who was sitting beside a gas heater trying to keep warm and a blast of accordion music and cold air enveloped us as we stepped into a small, well-packed hall decorated with multi-coloured Christmas lights and paper decorations.

At the back, on a raised stage with a scrawny Christmas tree, were three musicians – a young boy of about sixteen, playing a small set of drums, an older boy on guitar and a lady, probably their mother, on accordion.

They were playing Irish dance music, which was being listened to but not danced to by the mostly middle-aged audience.

"It's freezing in here," Annette said, despite the fact that she had not removed her coat and had moved close to me to capture any loose heat escaping from my body.

"You'll be alright when we start dancing," I said and put my arm around her shoulder. "Would you like an orange drink?"

"No, it's too cold."

All the chairs around the walls were occupied so we stood

where we were, just inside the door until the music stopped. The three musicians acknowledged the polite applause and left the stage.

"Why did we come here?" Annette asked, her teeth almost chattering with the cold.

"We never came the last time," I said. "By the time we moved to Tallaght this place had been turned into a billiard hall, but we heard so much about it that I thought it would be fun to see what all the fuss was about. It was supposed to be a great place."

She looked at me with disdain. "And is it?"

I smiled back weakly as she shivered. "Nope, another of the myths of the good old days bites the dust. Would you like to go?"

"Yes, but you've just paid in. Will you get your money back?"

I took her hand, and as we turned to leave the hall smiled at her and in my best John Wayne accent said, "The hell we will, come on let's get out of this joint."

We breezed past the man sitting by the gas heater as he looked at us and asked, "Leaving already?"

"Yes, but don't worry," I told him. "We'll be back when The Square opens."

He looked at us, puzzled, as we went back out into the cold night air and jumped into the car before heading back to town where we danced to Dickie Rock and The Miami showband at the Crystal, on Ann Street.

Chapter twenty

IT was now 1965, the year we first met in another time line, but in this timeframe we were already engaged.

After the proposal in the Shangri–La in December '63 Annette had chosen the ring the following year on her 18th birthday, in August, '64 and I was amazed to see how like the ring she wore the last time it was – a solitaire diamond mounted on a white gold/platinum band.

But overall this was a whole new life compared to the one I remembered and both of us were experiencing it all for the first time. I explained all this to Annette and it went some way to easing the anxiety I knew was still a problem for her. I was a different person to the one I had been the last time, I was more outgoing and confident, arrogant even, and not so easily impressed by the achievements of others. I was not slow to express my opinions about people, probably because I knew my opinions were right as they were informed by my knowledge of future events in the world, but I did not use that knowledge to try and change things. I let them take their own course as I knew they would, principally because I did not want to change things between Annette and me, more than I already had.

Annette was also different, but not so much that I was not as much in love with her as I had ever been in that past life. I put a lot of that difference down to me appearing in her life the way I did. What young girl would not be affected by someone telling them, and being able to prove it, that they had been married with three children in a previous life? She was also different in so far as she was pragmatic about our lives together – the one that was gone and the one about to begin, which she now believed she had more control over because of the way our relationship had developed.

But in all other ways she was the same person I remembered and loved from our previous time. She was still a very caring and compassionate person, still very spiritual with a strong commitment to her faith, and a desire to help others whenever she could. She was straight talking and honest with an innocence that was disarming – all the attributes that I had admired and loved her for in our past life.

Our relationship was improving all the time and we were spending a lot of time together and in the company of our families. Annette and my mother were getting on better than I ever expected them to and Annette even remarked on how fond she was of ma and how much she was looking forward to being her daughter-in-law.

My mother was confiding in Annette things about the family she never told me, though having been down this road before I had to pretend to be surprised when Annette mentioned certain things to me.

One thing I was genuinely surprised about was when Annette told me that my mother seemed very curious about how and when we met. It always came up at some point in any conversation they had, she said, and it was as if ma did not believe what we had told her and was trying to see if our story remained consistent with each telling.

We had decided to say that we had met first when Annette was on a school trip in Bray, but that we had seen each other once or twice a year or two later when I was working in Burroughs & Watts and Annette was working as an apprentice in O'Dea's. We said we used go to the same little shop in the morning to get the milk and cakes for the morning break in work and began talking. We started going out together then.

This story seemed to satisfy everyone else who asked how we met and it was plausible, but for some unknown reason my mother seemed reluctant to buy it. Why, I had no idea, but I did not dwell on it too much as otherwise everything else seemed to be going so well for us.

One of the things I was enjoying in this new life was the experience of driving Annette on trips around the country whenever the weather was fine and we had the time to do so. It was on one of those country drives that something from the past cropped up, which gave me great hope that this time around I could do something to prolong Annette's life and it need not necessarily end the same as the last time.

One Sunday in late May we went for a drive to Glendalough and after a great day walking around the lakes we went to the hotel for something to eat and drink. I had noticed Annette, from time to time, lagging behind but I did not think too much of it as I knew she liked to savour the countryside and meditate while she walked.

When we entered the hotel and found a table in the restaurant which we then sat at, she sighed and her breathing was laboured. I got her a glass of water and asked if she was alright, to which she replied that she felt very tired – exhausted even. This was unusual as we had not walked that far, or indeed that fast, and as I looked closely at her I noticed that she was very pale and drawn, I also noticed that what at first I thought had been my imagination was in fact true, she had lost weight. Annette had never been fat, or anything like it, but recently when I was holding her I had begun to be able to feel her ribs. All at once I remembered that when I met Annette the last time she was just out of hospital having been in St James's being treated for anaemia.

"I know what's wrong with you," I quickly said. "You're anaemic."

"And how do you know that Dr Halpin?" she asked with a smile.

"When I met you the last time you were not long out of hospital and you told me you had been in St James's because you were anaemic."

"You never told me that before," she replied.

I ignored that and just said, "You'll be alright, but you'll have to go and see a doctor and get it treated. It won't affect the wedding, by August you'll be ok. I know that for sure."

"Will I have to go into hospital?" she asked.

"I don't know. Maybe we caught it early and that won't be necessary this time."

My mind went racing ahead then, thinking if that is so maybe we can catch the Cancer earlier too this time and... It was something positive to think about. I then, to ease her mind and stop her worrying needlessly, told her all she had told me in the previous life about her Anaemia, which was not a lot as Annette tended to make light of it once she was better.

After a cup of coffee and a sandwich she seemed satisfied with what I had told her and after another short walk around the old cemetery and round tower we drove home.

Annette promised me that she would go to the doctors the next day, but would not hear of me going with her. She said her mammy would go.

The next day after work I wasted no time in getting out to Ballyfermot. I had a quick tea and washed and shaved, put on a clean shirt, drove as fast as was safe to do so and was on Annette's doorstep by 7pm. Annette opened the door when I knocked, and as she pulled the door closed behind her causing me to step down a step off the porch, she wrapped her arms around me.

"I'm anaemic," she cried into my hair.

"I know," I tried to say as she pressed my head to her breast. Loathe and all as I was to do so I gently eased myself free of her embrace, and stepping up a step took her in my arms and said, "There's nothing to worry about, you've been down this road before and you're going to be alright. I can promise you that with 100% certainty, everything is going to be fine. By August you'll be healthier than you've ever been."

"But Dr O'Brien said my blood was very low, that I was lacking in iron and that I'd have to go on a course of iron supplements," she cried.

"That's alright, there's nothing to worry about," I told her. "You did all that before. Did he say anything about you having to go into hospital?"

"No, he just said that I was to take the iron tablets and go back to him in a week."

"Well, that's exactly what you're going to do then, and maybe this time it will not be necessary for you to go into hospital at all. You might be getting treatment earlier than you did the last time. You never did tell me, or at least I don't remember if you did, when you went to see about it the last time."

She was a bit more composed then and said, "Come on in while I get ready."

I went into the front room with her where Liam and her sisters were looking at the television with Mary and Bill.

"Did she tell you?" Mary asked when I entered the room.

"Yes," I said. "She did, but listen to me, there's nothing for you to worry about, she's going to be fine, so don't think you're going to get out of paying for the wedding just yet."

I sat with the family watching television until Annette was ready, which was about ten minutes, and when she came back downstairs she was wearing a black and white striped blouse, open at the neck with a gold cross and chain. Her long auburn hair was loose and cascading around her shoulders and her legs were protruding from a waist-hugging black mini skirt, which ended just above her knees.

She looked fantastic and all I could say when I saw her was, "If you look this good sick there'll be no living with you when you're healthy."

Liam, on hearing this turned to Marie who was sitting beside him and mockingly said "yuk."

Annette made a mock lunge at him with her scarf and picking up her coat from the chair before saying to Mary and Bill, "We won't be late, but if we are don't wait up."

As we drove down Le Fanu Road I said, "About the anaemia, I know it's caused by a lack of iron and Dr O'Brien has given you iron tablets to take, but you can boost the power of the tablets by starting to take a glass or two of Guinness every day. It's full of iron and it will be good for you, it will also put back on the weight you've lost, so I was thinking that maybe we might go somewhere and you can try a glass and see if you like it."

"I don't like Guinness, only the cream on the head," she quickly replied. "I've tasted it at home, it's very bitter, I don't think I could drink it every day."

"But it would do you good," I persisted, "maybe even save you from having to go into hospital, and now that I think of it you did drink it before. After the babies were born you used to take a glass for a while, it helped you when you were breastfeeding. I'm sure the babies loved it, who wouldn't want to drink Guinness that way?"

She laughed at this and said, "I think I know someone who would."

I just squeezed her leg with my left hand, smiled and said, "So do I."

"Keep your mind on the road," she laughed. The added, "Maybe it's like you said and we caught it early and I won't have to go into hospital. I only took two tablets today and I feel better already. I don't feel as tired as I did yesterday at all."

We were now in Parkgate Street and I said to Annette, "Well, where do you want to go?"

"Why don't we go somewhere we... You used to go before and you can tell me all about it." she said.

"Do you mean that?" I replied somewhat surprised.

"Yeah, why not?" she said and squeezed my hand on the steering wheel.

"In that case I know just the place," I said and continued down the quays. "A place I know for a fact that you drank Guinness in before. We were there with your mother the night Ireland won the Eurovision for the first time and you were pregnant on David. You had a few glasses of Guinness that night in anticipation of the feeding requirements of our soon to be born son. So what better place to start drinking it again?"

"Did Ireland win the Eurovision?" Annette said in surprise.

"That's all in the future, nothing to get excited about just yet," I told her. "When the time comes again I'll tell you and you can put a few pounds on it and buy something nice for yourself with your winnings." Then laughing I added, "Stick with me babe and I'll make you a rich woman."

"That would not be fair," she said ."It would be like robbing money from the bookies."

"Ahhhh," I mocked. "The poor bookies! Sure God help them, they need all the money they can lay their hands on to keep them from having to retire to the poor house."

When we reached the five lamps I drove around to the side of Buckingham Street, just around the corner from Burke's pub, and parked the car. We walked the short distance to the entrance to the bar and went up the stairs to the lounge.

This was very close to where we used live in Clinches Court in the '65 timeframe.

It was Monday night so the lounge was almost empty, only two or three other people were sitting at the line of tables. We sat at a table with our backs to the window, facing the bar. When Annette had taken off her coat and laid it on an empty chair facing her I went to the bar, which was manned by a man in his late forties or early fifties, and asked for a pint and a glass of Guinness. As I was fumbling in my pocket for the money to pay for the drinks I noticed the barman, as he was pulling the drinks, glancing over at Annette. I let him know that I had noticed him, and turning my head did the same before turning back to the barman and smiling in satisfaction.

I brought the drinks over to the table and placed them in front of Annette and said, "The big one is yours."

"Oh, Andy. I don't think I'll be able to drink that."

She laid the glass back on the table without touching it and took a packet of cigarettes from her bag. She then reached for the glass of Guinness and put it under her nose and smelled it before making a face. She was about to put it to her lips when I took it from her and said, "Ah, Ah, not just yet, you have a little ritual to perform first. You used to love to drink the cream from my pint when we went out, so

197

for old time's sake let's continue the custom. Go on it will do you good," and I held my pint for her so she could put her mouth to the rim and drink the cream.

When she had tasted the cream she licked it from the side of her mouth and said, "That's lovely, if it was all like that I'd have no bother drinking it."

"I knew you'd like it," I said and wiped a tear from my eye as my mind raced back to another time.

"You used to do that all the time and I never thought I'd ever experience the joy and pleasure it gave me again, but what you just did was like going back to the future for me."

"Back to the future? I thought you could only go forward to the future," Annette said.

"That will be the name of a film, a few years from now."

"What will?" she asked.

"*Back to the Future.* That will be the name of a very popular film, and what you just did brought me back to my future, you used to do that all the time." I said as memories came flooding back.

Annette saw my reaction and reached for my hand and said, "Our future better be as good as you keep telling me it was or I'm going to be very disappointed."

I put my arm around her, pulled her close to me and as the barman looked over at us, I kissed her full on the lips and said, "Our future is going to be something beyond belief."

We settled back into our positions on the long wall seat facing the bar and I said to Annette, as she seemed reluctant to drink her Guinness, "Put down that cigarette and try a mouthful of it. You'll like it, remember when you drank wine for the first time, after the second mouthful you couldn't get enough of it."

She gave me a mock punch on the arm and said, "Don't be telling lies, I only drink wine to be sociable."

I laughed as I looked at her and said, "Of course you do, but we all know how much you like to be sociable."

And then, "Go on, have a go, it really will do you good, and you might not have to go into hospital."

This comment brought us back to reality and Annette took a sip from the glass, made a face and shook her head as the taste penetrated her taste buds and said, "Oh that's bitter."

"That's my girl" I said, "drink that up and I'll get you another one."

"I'll be doing well to finish this one," she replied and placed the glass back on the table and took a pull from her cigarette to disguise the taste of the beer in her mouth. We sat in silence for a few moments as we surveyed our surroundings and then Annette spoke, "How long was I in hospital for?"

"I honestly don't know. It was before I met you and you did not tell me about it until long after we were going out together. By that time you were better and well over it so it did not matter, but I don't think it was long, a week or two probably. Look Annette don't be worrying about it, you know that even if you have to go into hospital that everything will be alright, you'll survive to live a long..."

Suddenly I stopped talking and she looked at me.

"How did I die?"

I took her hand in mine"You're not going to die for a long, long time. We have lots to see and do yet, lots of living to do before that, and remember it may not be the same this time."

"But I did die, that's why you're here now isn't it?" she said almost accusingly.

"Everyone dies, nobody lives forever," I said matter of factually, trying to minimise the impact the conversation was beginning to have.

"Maybe you do, maybe you keep coming back to live your life over and over again," she said and her eyes seemed to look straight through me.

Momentarily I was caught off guard by what she had said and the way she had said it, startled and frightened by its implications. I tried to compose myself and not let her see that she had unnerved me.

"Don't be silly, Annette," I began to bluster. "What happened to me is just a freak occurrence, I must have been in the wrong place when some shift in the atmosphere happened and I was somehow thrown back in time."

"Maybe, but wasn't it convenient that you were thrown back to this time where you say you wanted to be? Where you say we were married before and lived as husband and wife and you have the knowledge to know that I died?"

Her mood had suddenly darkened and I was at a loss for words.

"I want to know how and when I died, I have a right to know that." she continued.

"Please Annette. Not now, this is not the time for that."

"And when is the time? When you decide it is? It's my life we're talking about and you have no right to play God and decide when I should know something as important as when I'm going to die. I want to know now... or there'll be no wedding, I mean that."

I was gobsmacked, I did not see this coming at all. I had thought I had handled that delicate situation well up to this and that Annette had managed to handle what I had told her about the future very philosophically as well; but it was obvious now that this knowledge she had about her death was proving to be tougher to handle than either of us had thought. This conversation was going to places I never intended when we came out this evening and I felt I was losing control of the situation.

I could see Annette's point, I had no right to withhold what I knew about her death from her, but that was in the last timeframe and I really did not know if the same thing would happen again in this timeframe.

All that was happening now had not happened the last time and even if the symptoms of Cancer did begin to manifest themselves again I knew that I would act sooner and get her treatment to try and prevent the same outcome as the last time. That had been my plan all along, to monitor the situation as we came closer to 2008 and at the first indication that history was beginning to repeat itself get Annette to a doctor.

I reached for her hand and in an effort to regain some degree of control said, "This is a different life for both of us. Things are happening now that never happened the last time. The same set of circumstances may not prevail this time and it would be wrong of me to, as you put it "play God" and tell you you were going to die at any particular time. I really don't know when you're going to die this time."

Annette shot back a retort immediately, "The same circumstances are prevailing. I'm anaemic now aren't I? Just like you told me I was at the same time in the other life."

"But that's just my point," I said almost jubilantly. "You had just come out of hospital when I met you the last time and that was August, which means your anaemia must not have been detected until much later than now. This is only May and already, because I knew you had anaemia before, you are already being treated. By my knowing you were anaemic we may have prevented you having to go into hospital this time. Likewise with your death. I know when and how it happened and by my knowing, if the same circumstances

201

begin to occur again I can prevent it happening this time. That's why I don't want to talk about it. I don't want you having to carry a worry in your head about something that is not going to happen because if it ever does, it is now preventable because I know about it. It's better you don't know the hows or whys of the situation. But I will promise you this, if the circumstances of your passing cannot be altered, I will tell you when that time comes, that's a solemn promise – but one I hope I will not have to keep."

What started out as an enjoyable evening was now looking like it was all going to end in tears.

"You're not serious about calling off the wedding are you?"

She just sat staring into the distance and had, by this time, only drank about half of the glass of Guinness. My pint was almost finished so I said that I was going to have another and asked her if she wanted anything. But she just stubbed the out her cigarette, took another one from the packet, lit it and replied, "I don't want another glass of Guinness, I'll have a red wine... please."

I went to the counter and ordered the drinks and when I came back Annette seemed a bit calmer. I placed the drinks on the table and smiled at her as I sat beside her.

"Try that wine, it's Spanish, you always liked Spanish wine," I said trying to put some distance between the exchange that had gone before.

"Thanks," is all she said.

Nothing was said again for a few moments as we both sat with our thoughts contemplating what had been said. Then as a means of breaking the silence I turned to Annette and said, "Annette, about the wedding, please don't call it off. I love you and I know you love me, please give this a chance. This is a love that has crossed the barriers of time and there must be a reason for that. It must have been meant to continue, maybe it was not finished when you passed away the last time and we've been given the chance to bring it to its natural conclusion this time, so please don't call off the wedding. It was a huge mistake on my part to tell you y... well I'm so sorry to have burdened you with that knowledge, but it does not mean it will happen this time. I think... I know and believe I can prevent it happening in the same way again, so please give me the opportunity to prove it."

She remained silent, no doubt pondering what I had just said, then she turned to me and said, "Andy, I'm finding this... this life that you know so much about and I know so little very hard to cope with. You came into my life four years ago, when I was little more than a school girl, with a fantastic story about you having been married to me in another lifetime, and to be completely honest with you I was frightened by what you were saying. I, at first, thought you were some kind of…well some kind of mad person wanting to attach yourself to me for God knows what purpose. But when the things you were saying began to become reality, my reality, like us moving to Ballyfermot and my daddy getting the job in International Saws and mammy becoming pregnant and calling the babies the names you said she would – and especially you knowing that I had moles on my back and stomach, something you could not possibly have know unless you had seen them, I had to consider the possibility that you were telling the truth.

"You obviously believed what you were saying and you were sincere in saying it and I came to believe you and trusted you, and I fell in love with you. I do love you Andy and I cannot imagine what my life would be like without you now. The things you have told me about our life together previously, well I can sometimes almost believe that I have a memory of that life too and I want to relive it all again with you. But you telling me that I died in that lifetime and you knowing how and when it will all happen again, well it confuses and frightens me, and there are times when I'm almost panic-stricken wanting to know the details. Then I convince myself that I don't need to know, that like you say this time it may be different, but I don't want to get married with that uncertainty hanging over me, I want the issue resolved. I want to go into this marriage without that worry on my mind, can you not understand that?"

I listened to her and knew she was right. Her passing and the circumstances of her passing would always be a blockage between us. It would have to be resolved before we got married or it would, I knew, prevent us leading the life of love and trust I knew we were capable of leading.

As long as it remained unresolved we would not be able to move forward together as equals and come anyway close to leading the life I had crossed the barriers of time to lead, and the life Annette had a right to lead.

I was faced with a dilemma that only I could resolve and I decided that I now had no more wiggle room – I had to tell her the whole truth, so I put my arms around her and whispered into her ear, "Tomorrow, I'll tell you all tomorrow."

Chapter twenty one

I DID not sleep well that night when I eventually got home and to bed. After I drove Annette back to Ballyfermot I promised her again that I would call and collect her and tell her all tomorrow. I then drove to Bohernabreena Cemetery, to the place my wife, the Annette of 1965, was buried.

My mind was besieged with worry over what I had done in telling Annette that she had passed away in a previous life and seeing the effect that it now had on her. I had no one to turn to for help and advice about what I should do. It would always have been Annette I would turn to in times of difficulties, but that was not possible now.

It was the first time I had been to the cemetery since my return to this time. I had thought of coming once or twice but had never done so, because it seemed I had no reason to, but now I had. I needed my wife's help and this was the only place I could think I might find it.

It was so different to the way I remembered it. There was mostly only fields from Tallaght Village all the way down the Old Bawn Road, and The Mill was once again the old thatch roofed pub, Brigid Burkes, on the junction of the Old Court and Ballinascorney Roads. Where there had been houses in 2010 there was only hedging and fields now.

I had drove up the Ballinascorney Road, the old country road that led to the cemetery, turning left and passing the semicircle of county council cottages and I parked just beyond Beasley Lodge, which in 2010 was a monumental sculptors.

I sat for a few moments in the car, contemplating my situation before getting out and walking to the cemetery entrance. I then pushed open the small iron gate and entered the cemetery, immediately glancing upwards to the mountain ahead of me, where looming against a backdrop of a clear star-filled sky was The Hell Fire Club.

I lowered my gaze from the old ruin that seemed to have cast a sinister shadow over my two lives and walked along the grass pathway with the few graves that were in the cemetery on the hill to my right, and headed straight down to what was only a field, but in 2010 was Annette's resting place.

The brightness of the night enabled me to see that there were far fewer graves than when I was here last. The cemetery was mostly fields of high grass. I walked to where I estimated Annette's grave would have been and did what I had done so many times before – I stood and cried for my loss.

I don't know what I expected of this visit, but as I stood in the silent empty cemetery at what would, if the same set of circumstances prevailed, be mine and Annette's last resting place, I felt no sense of panic or foreboding at this prospect, only a sense of peace and calm.

This was a good place to rest. Then I did what I had done many times before and sat down on the grass in front of what would be our grave and spoke to Annette. I knew she was not buried here yet but I had to talk to the Annette of the last life and this was the one place I felt I could do that.

When she passed away and I wanted advice and comfort this is where I came, this is where I found solace and consolation and a renewal of faith that whatever was troubling me would soon pass and that all would be well, she never failed me.

Now I wanted her to help me handle the situation I had got myself into and help me tell the eighteen-year-old Annette how she passed over.

After about thirty minutes of silent communication during which I believed the Annette of 1965 did indeed communicate with me, as I could hear in my mind her oft spoken words, "All Is Well" so I stood up and after plucking and placing a few wild flowers on the place our grave would be one day I made my way back to the gate.

Although it was late when I eventually got home my mother was still up. She was sitting at the fire nursing a cup of tea. I did not want to talk about the events of the night so I just took off my jacket and placing it on a chair bid her good night and was about to go on up to bed when she spoke and said, "It's very late, where were you till this hour?"

"With Annette," I replied and was about to open the door when my mother spoke again. "Until this hour, it's almost two o'clock!"

"We were talking," I said.

"Is there anything wrong?" she asked, in a tone that suggested there was.

"No we were just talking," I replied not wishing to go into any more details than was necessary.

"You must have an awful lot to talk about," she said, almost willing me to confide in her.

I did not reply to her comment, I just said I was tired and wanted to go to bed.

"Would you like a cup of tea before you go up?" she asked.

"No," I replied and was about to open the door when a

thought flashed through my mind and I hesitated. I had already noticed how much more perceptive and pragmatic this woman was compared to my mother in the last life and something in my mind seemed to be telling me to talk to her now. I looked at the woman sitting on the armchair nursing a cup of tea and in her eyes I could see pools of wisdom just waiting to be fished. I pushed the door shut and came back into the room.

"OK, I will have a cup of tea," I said.

She placed her cup on the ledge of the fireplace and getting up off the chair said, "Sit down so and I'll make a fresh sup."

I collapsed into the small sofa facing the window, kicked off my shoes and with my legs stretched out under the table put my hands behind my head and sighed.

"You sound weary," my mother called from the kitchen. "Just tired," I said.

"I suppose all the wedding arrangements and buying the house is exhausting," she replied.

"Yeah, it is," is all I said, and closed my eyes.

I started to nod off and then I heard my mother come out of the kitchen with a cup of tea in her hand and place it on the table in front of me. She also placed a sandwich on a plate on the table as well. Through my sleepiness I heard her say, "There's your tea."

I moved from the sofa to a chair at the table and my mother brought out a cup of fresh tea for herself and sat at the table beside me.

"Thanks," I said as I took a bite from the sandwich.

"Is everything alright between you and Annette?"

"Yes, of course it is, why wouldn't it be?"

"You seem preoccupied about something. Is there something on your mind, anything you're worried about? she asked me.

"Why would I be worried about anything? Everything is arranged and the house is on schedule," I said.

"Well if there is anything you're worried or concerned about don't be afraid to talk about it, to Annette, or if you like to me. Don't go into the marriage with something on your mind that is unresolved or it will be hanging over you all the time and that can lead to problems later on."

I looked at this woman, who in so many ways was not the woman who had been my mother in the last life. She was so perceptive, and I wondered what was going on in her mind and if she knew or suspected something that she was keeping to herself.

I wondered should I draw her out and see just what knowledge she was the custodian of. Should I even confide the truth of my situation to her. I remained silent as I contemplated what I should do and she waited for a response to her invitation to talk. When I was not forthcoming with any response, however, she finished her tea and stood up from the table, saying, "Well if you don't want to talk I think I'll go to bed."

She went into the kitchen to wash her cup and I thought about telling her of my predicament. I opened my mouth to speak and called to her, "Ma…"

"Yes" she replied and came back out of the kitchen, standing expectantly at the door. But I bottled it and just said, "Goodnight Ma," and went up to bed.

Joe was fast asleep in the big double bed in the front bedroom so I did not turn on the light, I stripped myself down to my underpants and lay on top of the covers. The events of the night not allowing me the luxury of sleep. I had told Annette I would tell her everything the next day, but how I was going to do that I did not know.

This reprise of our life was not going the way I had

209

expected it would, this was a completely new and so far unlived life compared to the one I was expecting. I was a different person to the person I had been, but I suppose that was only to be expected with all the knowledge I had brought with me into this life, but the difference in Annette and especially in my mother was something I had not expected. How things would progress from here on was now worrying me, it definitely would not be as it was before, that I knew for certain.

My mother was the big surprise of this life, a completely different woman, more confident and knowledgeable than the woman I remembered. Tonight I even felt that she knew much more about my situation than she should – that she was holding back, waiting for me to open the door to allow her enter into my world, and I almost did.

I needed help badly to guide me through the time maze I had entered, even from my mother. Tomorrow I had to tell Annette how she died and I did not know how to do that. While these thoughts were racing through my head I heard my mother climb the stairs and go into the back bedroom where my father was sleeping. I did not sleep at all that night and I was still awake when the first light of the new day began to chase the darkness from the room and I heard my father getting up to go to work.

After I heard him going out and the hall door being closed I got out of the bed, being careful not to wake my still sleeping brother, and put my trousers on before knocking on the door of the back bedroom. I went in to find my mother lying awake in the bed.

"Do you feel like talking now?" she asked as if she knew this moment was coming.

I stood at the door and gently closed it behind me.

There was a chair beside the bed with some clothes on it

and my mother reached over to it and took a cardigan from it, knocking the rest of the clothes onto the floor. As she sat up into a sitting position she put the cardigan around her shoulders and said to me, "Sit down there."

I did as I was told and sat on the chair.

"Well, what's on your mind?" she asked as I sat in silence on the chair trying to gather my thoughts.

"I don't know…I mean, I…Do you ever get the feeling that things have happened before? I eventually managed to say.

"Do you?" she replied, which was not the answer I expected or wanted to hear.

"Sometimes," I said after a moment or two.

"Is that what you want to talk about? Is that what's on your mind, things that have happened before?"

"Yes," I timidly replied.

"Like what, what has happened before?" she pressed me. Before answering that I had to think just how much should I say, how much should I tell her without making her think I was unstable and not in the whole of my senses. So I decided to probe her a little bit first to see if I could ascertain if my judgement of her heightened perceptions was correct or not, and to try and find out exactly where she was coming from with her questions.

"Ma," I said, "Do you remember a few years ago when we were in the Phoenix Park, you, me and Joe and I rolled down the hill near the gate and I was lying on the ground when you called me to go home?"

"Yes," she replied instantly and without hesitation.

"Did you see me rolling down the hill, I mean actually see me rolling?"

"Yes," she again replied without hesitation.

"And did you see me before I rolled down the hill?" I

continued, not knowing really where I was going with this line of questioning but wanting to see if I could get any information from her that would help me understand how I got there from 2010.

"Yes," she again replied in a manner that invited another question, so I accepted her implied invitation and asked, "What was I doing immediately before rolling down the hill?"

She sat up straight in the bed pulled the cardigan around her shoulders looked straight at me and said, "You were talking to a man, an elderly man."

As she spoke these words she kept her gaze firmly on me. "A man?" I asked with surprise. "What was he like? Who was he? Did I know him?"

"He was about sixty or so and he was wearing dark trousers and a very modern, light coloured, American type of jacket with an emblem of some kind and a zip up the front. I don't know if you knew who he was or not. Did you?" She waited for me to digest the information.

My God! She was describing me, me as a sixty five-year-old man, the me who walked into the park and let his imagination travel back to his boyhood. Was I talking to myself?

"What else happened? What else did you see?" I hastily asked her as I tried to remember all I did before rolling down the hill.

"When I saw you talking to the man I was on my way over to you to see if there was anything wrong, but before I reached you, both of you, you and the man, lay on the ground and rolled down the hill," she said, and waited for my reaction.

"The two of us rolled down the hill?" I asked incredulously.

"Yes, the two of you" she confirmed and her eyes bore into mine.

"But, but... Ma... where did he go? The man I mean, I didn't see him with me at the bottom of the hill."

"No, he was gone. He was not anywhere to be seen when you stopped rolling at the bottom of the hill. I did not see where he went. It was as if you both merged into each other and there was only you left at the bottom of the hill. Do you not remember talking to him, what he said to you? Do you not remember that?" she asked.

"No, no I don't remember anything like that," I said mystified.

"How long were we talking, me and this man?" I then asked her.

"I don't know, I was talking to a woman before I saw you, and then you were talking for about five minutes before I began to go over to you. I thought there might have been something wrong. The next thing you were both rolling down the hill."

I remained silent as I tried to come to terms with and make sense of what my mother had told me. I was positive there was no one else apart from the ghosts of my childhood that my imagination had conjured up in the park that day. I certainly didn't remember talking to anyone, least of all a young boy.

"What were you talking about, you and the man?" I heard my mother say, breaking my reverie.

"I don't know, I don't remember talking to a man," I absently replied.

"A change came over you after that day, you began to act very strange. It was almost as if you became an adult overnight, and you said something the next day that I can still recall. You were up early and did not go to work but went out somewhere and when I asked where you were going you said to me that you were going to see... my daughter-in-law."

"Yes," I said. "I remember that day."

"Were you going to see Annette that day?" she asked, and I felt a chill run down my spine.

"Yes I was, I was going to see Annette."

"Was that the first time you met Annette, or had you known her before?" she asked. "Is that what you meant when you spoke of things happening again? Had you known Annette before?"

I looked at my mother as she sat in the bed waiting for an answer. I knew she would not be able to comprehend and I ran my hands through my hair, closed my eyes and said, "Yes, yes I had met Annette before, a long, long time ago and I did not think I would ever see her again, but something happened to me that day in the park, which enabled me to be with her again."

"What happened, do you want to tell me about it?" she replied and reached over and took my hand.

"I don't think you would understand," I said.

"Why not tell me anyway? It will do you good just to talk about it, and sure even if I don't understand, by talking about it to someone it might help you understand it a bit better yourself." She said this in a way that made it sound almost therapeutic to do so.

"Yes," I replied. "Maybe it will."

I then looked at this wise woman and decided to plunge straight into it.

"Ma, I've been here before. What I mean is I've lived before. In another time Annette and I were married. Things I should only be doing for the first time I've done before. Can you understand that? Is that possible?"

She said nothing in response to my statement and I thought she was confused and did not understand what I was trying to tell her, but then she said, "Andrew, I had a very strange dream a short time before you rolled down the hill in the park. In the dream I knew I was dead, but I could see you as a grown man, you were sitting in a pub or restaurant with a lot of strange people, people I did not know, and I knew that something terrible was going to happen to you, but I did not know what. I wanted to help you, to warn you about this thing that was going to happen, but I did not know what it was. I was confused. I tried to speak to you but you could not hear me. I was then directed by a very bright light to a woman in the room, a woman I did not know, but in my mind someone was telling me that if I told this woman what I wanted to say to you she would tell you.

She paused for a moment then continued, "But I still did not know what to say, only that I would be there for you when this terrible thing happened. I told the woman this and I told her who I was and to tell you what I was saying. I then had an image of you kneeling at a grave plucking thorns from a rose and I told the woman to tell you that. And then I saw the name on the headstone..."

"Whose name was on the headstone?" I asked, knowing what the answer to my question would be before she answered.

"Annette Halpin," she replied.

I was shattered by what I was hearing and after shedding a few tears I said, "I remember that night, it was the night of the 12th anniversary of your passing in my last life and I was in a hotel in Tallaght with Annette and some other people when a woman I did not know came over to me and said things which at the time had no meaning and I did not understand. Later on, when Annette became ill with Cancer what the woman said took on a new meaning. You were trying to warn me that our time together, Annette's and mine, was nearing the end of the earthly journey we had begun almost forty-four years before. I did not understand the warning at the time."

As I spoke these words tears were rolling down my mother's cheeks and I reached over to her and put my arms around her.

"You must have loved her very much for the strength of that love to break through the barriers of time so you could be with her again," she said through her tears.

"I do, I do," I cried into her hair.

We disengaged and as I wiped my tears in the hem of the bed sheet as I said, "You knew this all along?"

"I knew something strange had happened to you after that day in the park", she said, "but I dared not believe..."

Andrew the man, you were talking to in the park that day was the man you grew up to be, the same man I saw and tried to give a warning to about something I did not fully understand in my dream. That day in the Phoenix Park you, as an adult, were talking to yourself as a child. The only person who could allow you to travel back in time and be with Annette again."

I was stunned by what she was saying, despite everything that had happened it was scarcely believable that such a thing could happen or be possible. That I had changed places with myself, changed the old for the new and become young again in order to be with Annette once more.

"Then you know why I've been preoccupied," I said as soon as I began to realise the significance of the unbelievable event that had occurred, to allow me be with Annette again. "I missed Annette so much after she passed away and wanted to do it all over again that I somehow caused this to happen. I've had to convince Annette that we've been married before and that was not easy, but she accepts that now. During the course of that convincing process, however, I foolishly told her that she had passed away in the last life and she is threatening to call off the wedding unless I tell her how and when she passed. That is something I don't want to do because I've learned that not everything need necessarily be the same this time. You, for instance, are a completely different woman to what you were in my last life, and I may, when the time comes, be able to prevent Annette passing away at the same time in this lifetime."

"Why did you tell Annette she passed away?" my mother asked.

"I was foolish and thought I had no choice when she was putting pressure on me to tell her the truth of why I was here. She wanted full details of our life together and I was desperate to convince her that what I was telling her was the truth. She was only fourteen when I made myself known to her and I was so happy and excited at being with her again that I forgot that, and was still thinking of her as the mature woman she was when we were last together. She has made me promise that I will tell her all about her passing before she will agree to marry me, and last night I told her I would do that today – tell her with complete honesty, how and when she passed away." I was feeling low but glad I had unburdened myself at last of my secret.

"Then that's what you have to do. Be honest with her, but try to make her understand that because this life is not exactly as the last one was, the time and circumstances of her passing may not, and need not necessarily, be the same."

"Ma, that's what I'm trying to do, but it won't be easy, she got very upset last night. She's still very young and this kind of knowledge is not something she should have to be concerned with when she's about to get married."

"The last few years must not have been easy for you, and

217

trying to convince Annette that you came from the future, her future, must have been a very daunting task" she said.

"You do believe what I've told you don't you, that I've lived a life with Annette before?" I asked her, just so as to be sure I was not misinterpreting what she seemed to be saying.

"Yes, I believe you" she replied.

"Then, Ma," I said. "What happened to Andrew, the young me. What I mean is, where is he now?"

She sighed. "From what I saw in the Phoenix Park over four years ago, you, the man in my dream, happened to him. As far as I can see that is the only way time travel is possible, changing places with yourself in a different timeframe. How long this situation will last I do not know, it may or may not be permanent so make the most of it. The young Andrew may at some time wish as fervently and passionately as you did to once more resume his life in this time, so don't waste anymore time. Tell Annette what she wants to know and then do all the things you wanted to do and did not do the last time. Just don't do the things that caused you pain."

To say that I was surprised by our talk was the understatement of this, or any other century. I was in a complete state of shock as I came out of my mother's bedroom but I had also never been so grateful for her love.

It was because of her too, that I would face Annette and tell her what she needed to hear.

Chapter twenty two

I PICKED Annette up from work that evening with a somewhat sketchy idea of how I was going to tell her what I had to and we drove towards Tallaght/Bohernabreena, passing the cemetery and heading up the Ballinascorney Road towards the Dublin/Wicklow mountains.

Not much apart from small talk about the weather and little things that happened in work that day passed between us, both of us apprehensive about what lay ahead.

It was a lovely warm, bright, May evening and I parked the car at a spot overlooking the Waterworks where we used walk in another life. I wanted the place I would tell her about her passing to be as pleasant and tranquil as possible. We sat taking in the view and after a few minutes of unwinding our tensions, helped by the spectacular view below us, I said I was now prepared and ready to tell her what she wanted to know, so long as she was absolutely sure she wanted to hear it.

"Yes, I really want to know. Without that knowledge I can't move on. It would always be something I felt you were keeping from me, like a secret affair. It would always be the other woman in the bedroom," she replied, not looking at me as she spoke but gazing out over the lakes below us.

So this was it, I had come to the point of no return and just as surely as we were on the precipice of the mountain that plunged down to the lakes below us, I was on the precipice of something I had hoped to avoid.

As gently as I could I began to relate the circumstances of her passing to Annette, telling her of the first signs of the Cancer manifesting itself by her developing a sore throat after we came back from a cruise to Alaska, taken to celebrate our 40th wedding anniversary in 2008. I told her of her visits to the doctor and the antibiotics he prescribed, that did not have any effect on her sore throat. I told her about the two sets of X-rays also not showing anything wrong and her continuing to work right up to Christmas 2008. I told her about her not being able to swallow solid food at Christmas and of her going back to her doctor who at last became concerned enough to send her for a scan.

As a result of the scan, she was, I told her, admitted to St James's Hospital as an inpatient to verify and diagnose what the scan had discovered, a large tumour in her throat.

Every now and then I stopped and asked Annette if she wanted me to continue, the answer was always the same, "Yes, go on."

I told her of the confirmation of a cancerous tumour in her throat and of her having to have a tracheotomy performed. I had to explain to her what a tracheotomy was and recalling that truly awful procedure was like having to go through it all over again. I was finding talking about those terrible times very hard and wanted her to tell me to stop, but even as I was trying to compose myself and continued to relate the details to her she seemed determined to hear it all. I told her of the operation to remove the Cancer on the 20th of January 2009 and how it had failed because five hours into that operation the surgeon discovered the Cancer had spread to her Oesophagus and it was inoperable.

I rushed through the aftermath of the operation telling

her how well she recovered and the plans that were made for her to have a seven-week course of chemotherapy and radiation treatment in St Luke's Hospital after she was released from St James's on the 20th of February, exactly a month after her operation.

I told her how hopeful we all were that this treatment would work and the Cancer would be at least held at bay so she would be able to lead a near normal life, for how long we did not know; but seeing how well she had recovered from two heavy operations we had high expectations that it would be lengthy.

I wanted Annette to call a halt to my pain at having to go through all of this again and paused every now and then to give her the chance to say she had heard enough, but she did not do so, she just sat impassively staring into the distance and I was forced to continue. I was nearing the end of the narrative, coming to the most difficult part and I was desperate for her to tell me to stop. I did not want to go through that again, but as I hesitated she turned her face to me and said, "Continue on, I'm OK."

She may well have been OK, but I wasn't. I was going through hell all over again.

"David, Mina and I were with you on Holy Thursday in St Luke's, it was five weeks into your treatment," I continued. "We were waiting for the doctors to be ready to commence your treatment when you began to have trouble clearing mucus from the tracheotomy tube in your neck. This had been a problem before but we had been told it was not dangerous. A nurse came and cleared the blockage and you were alright again. David had to go and I remained with you in your room waiting for the doctor to come and examine you to determine if you were OK to have your chemo treatment. After the examination by the doctor he gave you the all clear as you seemed to have fully recovered after the distress of the blockage. He then left to get the "line" ready for the treatment, saying he would only be a few minutes. We were sitting on your bed and when the doctor left you turned to me and spoke the last words I ever heard from your mouth, "I think I'll go to the toilet before he starts," you said and got off the bed, walking out of my life."

I stopped speaking and tears flowed down my face as I relived the nightmare all over again. Annette squeezed my hand and I thought she had heard enough, but to my profound dismay she said, "Relax for a minute before you continue."

"Annette," I pleaded "I can't do this, I really can't."

"I want to know Andy, I want to know how I died. I can't move on until you tell me everything."

It was no use I had to go on, but I was not sure how much more of this torture I could endure as I again picked up the narrative.

"I remained sitting on the bed after you went into the toilet, and then after less than a minute I heard a loud bang on the toilet door. I jumped from the bed and pushed the door in and found you leaning on the hand basin unable to get your breath. I think, though I'm not sure, that I helped you out of the toilet as I called for help. What happened after that is muddled in my mind and I have no definite recollection. I can remember doctors and nurses crowding into the room and I was ushered out and left waiting in a room across the hall. I came out of that room at some point and I remember standing at the door of your room and seeing you surrounded by medics. You seemed to be unconscious and then I was put back into the room across the hall and the door to your room was closed to me. I had a mobile phone with me and I phoned David and told him what had happened. After a while, and I really don't know how long, a doctor came and told me that he thought you had had a cardiac arrest and that you were on a respirator. He said they proposed to turn the respirator off shortly and for me to be prepared for the consequences when they did – in other words he did not expect you to survive.

"I was so traumatised by what was happening that I did not even ask to be allowed to see you, I just remained in the room after the doctor was called back into your room. I was totally numb and alone and my faculties were not working. Then I heard a commotion outside and doctors and nurses were all over the place, I went out and tried to get back into your room but I was prevented from doing so by a nurse who was standing just inside the door. I was told to wait in the room across the hall."

I gulped. "Soon after the commotion ceased the doctor came into me again and said that you had been taken off the respirator but you were continuing to breath unaided and there was nothing more that could be done for you in St Luke's, so they were arranging for an emergency ambulance to bring you back to St James's. I was not allowed to travel with you in the ambulance because of all the equipment and ambulance personnel going with you, so a taxi was organised for me and I rang David again and told him the situation asking him to contact Gina and Robert and let them know what was happening. I also asked him to contact your sisters and tell them. I said I would meet them in the hospital. I got the taxi and met David at the hospital gate as he was going in. Gina and Robert were already at the hospital and had seen you being taken into the emergency department, they told us that you were unconscious when you were taken in.

I continued, "After being examined in the emergency

department you were transferred to a room in St John's ward in the main hospital and after a while we were all allowed to see you. By this time your sisters and brother Liam were there as well."

"Where was my mammy?" Annette then asked.

I told her that her mother was still alive in 2010 but she was confined to a nursing home on account of her age and health. I did not elaborate on her mother's condition as I was finding telling her about her own hard enough.

"Did my mammy know that I died?" she wanted to know, to which I just replied "no."

Again I tried to get Annette to call a halt but she insisted that she wanted to know it all.

"This is very hard for me," I pleaded. "It's like going through that awful time all over again do you really have to hear it all?"

"I have to," she replied without compassion, so I was forced to continue.

"The nurses and doctors made you as comfortable as possible and we, the family were with you all the time. We made your room cosy with flowers and candles and brought up a radio and CD player and we had soft soothing music fill the room. We played all the music we knew you liked and we played your own compositions hoping you were hearing it. We were not sure if you were as the doctors had told us that they thought you may have suffered brain damage when you went into the coma on Holy Thursday and that you may have been unconscious, but we hoped they were wrong.

"We discovered that they were in fact wrong in the early hours of Easter Sunday morning. A priest came to visit you late on Easter Saturday night and after he had said some prayers and gave you the last rites he left leaving just me and David with you. After a while you became a bit uneasy and I thought that you might be in pain so I asked you if you were, not knowing for sure if you could hear me but I got no response from you. I then asked you to try raising your little finger if you were in pain but again there was no response so I said if you were not in pain to try raising your little finger and immediately your little finger shot up.

"I was delighted to see that reaction because I knew that meant that you had not suffered brain damage as the doctors had thought and that you could hear and understand us. I really thought at that point that you would pull through and confound all the doctors who had at that point given up on you.

"When David had to leave I spent the rest of the night with you, talking to you and holding you, singing to you and telling you how much I loved you and how sorry I was for all the times I had hurt you and caused you pain. Much of what I was saying I know you heard, but as the night wore on you appeared to lapse back into a coma and I'm not sure if you were aware of what I was trying to say."

I paused again at this point, really distressed, but Annette just took my hand in hers and said, "I know this must be distressing for you and I would not ask you to tell me about unless it was truly necessary, but you really have to know that I can't move on from here unless I know everything. I can't start to live that life you've told me I've lived unless I know how it ended. I know it may seem foolish to you but my knowing how it ended I believe goes some way to giving me a degree of control over all the things you know about that life and I don't."

She then gently kissed me on the side of my face, wetting her lips in my tears and I continued the story.

"Over the next two days, Easter Sunday and Monday,

225

all your family and friends came to see you and say their goodbyes as you got weaker and slipped deeper into a coma. In the early hours of Easter Tuesday morning, at 4-21 a.m. with David, Robert, Gina and me by your side you quietly and peacefully passed away from us."

I was now sobbing uncontrollably, having to live again that terrible time and Annette was now comforting me with my head on her shoulder as she stroked my face and wiped my tears with a handkerchief.

"That's enough," I said through my tears. "I can't go on any more, I can't go through this again."

We sat in the car for about twenty minutes and the only sound to be heard was the sound of my sobs as Annette held me close to her. When at last I raised my head from her shoulder her hair was wet from the tears I had shed. "I'm glad you told me that," she said, as she continued holding me to her. "And I'm glad you came back to me."

"So am I, so very glad," I said, as I raised my lips to hers and we kissed passionately, our emotions overwhelming us.

We composed ourselves and Annette dried my tears. It was now almost dark and the mountains were casting shadows over the still lakes below us.

"We better go," I said. "It will be dark soon."

"Do we have to?" Annette said softly.

"I love you so much, you're so different" I said, as I, once again, tenderly pressed my lips to hers.

"And I love you" she replied, "You can finish the story tomorrow."

"What?!" I exclaimed as I pulled myself away from her embrace.

"That's it, that's all there is. I've told you everything."

"You haven't told me about my funeral and where you buried me."

"Please, Annette I can't go through all that again."

"Andy I need to know, I have to know. I can't just hear half of the story. I'll be forever wondering where you buried me. Just tell me where you buried me, that's all. I know you probably gave me a good funeral so if you just tell me where I was buried I'll be happy."

I was wrong I thought, about her being different, she was as tenacious and exacting about getting what she wanted as her earlier incarnation had ever been, exactly the same, and I loved her for it. I knew she would not let go on this and I would be better off satisfying her curiosity now as letting it go on any longer, so I stepped out of the car and as I stood in the darkness I asked her, "Would you like to see where you were buried?"

"Now?" she asked in surprise. "Is it near here?"

"Yes," I said. "Very. We can go there on our way back if you like."

"OK," is all she said in reply.

We finished dressing and I got back into the car and we drove in silence down the dark country road towards Bohernabreena Cemetery. We were there in a matter of minutes and I parked the car near the small iron gate I had entered the cemetery through the previous night. It was now pitch dark and there was not a light on the road, nor the sight or sound of another living thing. As far as the world was concerned we were the only ones in it. We both sat in the car when I parked it, neither of us making a move to get out.

I took Annette's hand in mine and asked, "Are you ready for this?"

She did not reply, but squeezed my hand and placed her other hand on the door handle. I released her hand, opened my door and stepped out of the car before walking around to her side and opening her door. I held it open, but she made no move to get out so after a few moments I gently closed the door and went back around to the driver's side and got into the car.

Without a word I turned the key in the ignition and pulled away from the cemetery gate.

"We can be married now," Annette said as we drove down the road, "my mind is at ease." And smiling she turned to me and said, "I've seen the future and it looks good."

She then kissed me on the side of the face as I was driving and said, "And I'm glad you buried me in the mountains, it's where I would have wanted to be laid to rest."

A tear escaped from my eye and in the voice of Annette of 1960 I could clearly hear the voice of Annette of 1965 giving her approval for the choice that was made for her, way back in another time; and in doing so fulfilling the words of a song she composed and which I had inscribed on her headstone for her birthday in August 2010.

"Beneath These Mountains, We're Going To Live Our Lives Forevermore."

Chapter twenty three

AFTER that night in May Annette never again mentioned anything about her passing in the previous timeframe. She recovered rapidly from the anaemia she had been suffering from and this time did not have to spend time in hospital, which was a great relief and a welcome sign that she need not necessarily succumb to the Cancer if it struck again in this lifetime.

We were now concentrating on the fast-approaching wedding in August and all our energies were directed to that. I was still not happy about living beneath the ruin of The Hell Fire Club but Annette loved the house and would not hear of a move anywhere else, so it was something I was going to have to get used to. It was a small price to pay, I reckoned, for having my wish for a second lifetime with Annette.

As we were not now going to meet for the first time on Bray Head on August Sunday we drove out there one fine Sunday near the end of June and I took Annette to the spot I had first laid eyes on her in another lifetime. It was a warm sunny day much like it was on the day we met. Bray was packed with day-trippers enjoying the sunshine as they walked along the prom or the more energetic of them made their way up the head.

After parking the car facing towards the sea near the Bray

Head Hotel we bought ice cream cones and I took Annette's hand as we walked in the direction I had taken in 1965 mark one. When we reached the spot I told Annette and we sat on the grass opposite where she had been sitting with her friend when I saw her for the first time. There was a group of teenage boys and girls sitting there laughing and talking and as I looked over at them I could not help but wonder would any of them be as lucky, this sunny weekend, as I had been all those years ago to form a loving relationship that would transcend the boundaries of time.

Everything was now going as smoothly between us as I had dreamed it would when I first saw Annette again in this lifetime in Newbridge in 1960 and she was even more beautiful now than she had been then.

The wedding was now only a matter of weeks away and all was ready, the church, the hotel, the honeymoon and the house. Annette was so happy now as well, she had put all the worry and stress about her passing behind her and she was really getting involved in everything to do with arranging the wedding. She even took charge of the tickets and passports, reminding me that I had lost them the last time and she wasn't taking any chances on that bit of history repeating itself. I had not seen her as happy in this lifetime.

My little secret was still that, a little secret, only Annette and my mother knew the strange story behind our wedding and the fact that we had done it all before, or at least I had done it all before.

I told Annette about my mother knowing a few days before the wedding. I had promised Annette that there would never be any secrets between us, and that's the way we intended to keep it, a closely guarded family secret with only me and the two women in my life in on it.

I did not know how Annette would react to hearing that

my mother knew our secret but they were bonding so well at this early stage of their relationship that Annette was relieved, I think, to know that she had an ally in my mother to share her secret with.

On the day before the wedding, a Saturday, I went down town and scoured jewellers shops until I found a Celtic necklace identical to the one I had bought for Annette for her 21st birthday, the last time, as I wanted to give her something very special as a wedding present and I also believed in the old proverb, something old, something new etc.

The necklace was both old and new and I wanted her to wear it on our wedding day. After I managed to find the one I wanted I got the shop assistant to gift wrap it and I inserted a card into it telling her how much I loved her while asking her to wear it at our wedding the following day, because there was a story behind it which I would tell her about on our honeymoon.

I wrote her name and address on the package and put it into the glove compartment of the car. I intended to surprise her by dropping it into her letterbox in Ballyfermot later that evening.

Before going home, I drove to the Phoenix Park, to the North Circular Road gate where my second life began almost five years ago. I sat in the car for a while going over and marvelling at all that had happened in that time, scarcely daring to believe it all.

I eventually got out of the car and walked to the railings just inside the People's Gardens and looked at the carpet of lush green grass spread out before me. There were some people in the park enjoying the fine weather and as I stood gazing at them I noticed an elderly man standing to my left under a tree. I was about to bid him good day when suddenly he began to approach me and I recognised him.

As my doppelganger approached he reached his arms out and clung to me before we fell to the ground and rolled down the hill.

*****

"Are you alright mister?"

I opened my eyes and I found myself staring into the concerned looking face of a park ranger who was kneeling beside me.

"Here, give me your hand and I'll help you up," he said as I looked at him totally confused.

When I was standing the ranger looked at me and said,"You're a bit old for that kind of thing aren't you?"

"What kind of thing?" I asked.

"Rolling down the hill, at your age, you might have injured yourself doing that. You're not a young fella any more you know," he said. "You're not hurt are you?"

"No, no, I replied, I'm alright, just a bit winded."

All of a sudden I became conscious of the fact that I was wearing the clothes I had been wearing in 2010 when I rolled down the hill and that I was not the young man I had been a few moments ago. I looked at myself, at my hands – I had my wedding ring on my finger. My stomach churned. I was an elderly man again!

"What year is this?" I asked the ranger in a near panic.

"It was 2010 when I got up this morning," he replied and eyed me suspiciously. "Are you sure you're alright?"

"Are you sure it's not 1965?" I almost pleaded.

"Did you hit your head when you rolled down the hill mister?"

I was not sure what was happening but I tried to quickly

compose myself so as not to arouse his suspicions further and I tried to smile as I replied, in what I hoped was a jocular way, "I'm alright, I was just hoping I had rolled back the years when I rolled down the hill."

He smiled and said, "Yeah, we all wish we could do that at times don't we, will you be alright getting home?"

"Yes, I'm fine," I said. Thanks for your help," and I walked back up to the top of the hill.

There was no sign of an old Cambridge car anywhere in sight. With my mind in turmoil I headed for the Luas and home. *What happened today? Was it all a hallucination? Or did my mind play a cruel trick on me in making me believe I had travelled back in time and been with Annette again?* It had all seemed so real, almost five years of the 1960s could not have been squeezed into a few minutes of 2010 – no it was too real for that, I had travelled back through time, I had been with Annette again. I wanted to believe that, with all my heart and soul I wanted it to be true; that somehow, if only temporary, my wishing and praying to be with Annette again had been powerful enough to allow me to cross the boundaries of time and space.

It was evening when I got home to Tallaght and when I turned the key in the door of the empty house and stepped into the hall I noticed an envelope on the floor. I picked it up and looked at it. It was addressed to Annette in what I recognised used to be my hand writing – before I became very careless.

It bore an old Irish stamp, the one with the map of Ireland resembling a teddy bear, and it had a post office franking date of December 1960. The envelope was faded and appeared to have been lying somewhere dusty for a considerable length of time.

There was a post office sticker on the back of the envelope, which said, *Sorry for the delay in delivering this letter, but it was only discovered in an old delivery bag when a cleanup of the store room was done a few days ago.*

I opened the envelope and gasped as I took out the Christmas card that I had sent to Annette, at our address in Tallaght, back in 1960.

I would cry no more.